DRAGON SIGHT: DARK FANTASY STORIES OF MAGIC, MURDER, & REVENGE

JACK CURRAN

HAWK'S FLIGHT PUBLISHING

JACK CURRAN

A SHORT STORY COLLECTION

DRAGON SIGHT

Published by Hawk's Flight Publishing.

Print ISBN: 978-1-7395868-7-4

Ebook ISBN: 978-1-7395868-6-7

Cover design by Miblart

Editing by Mel: https://www.getproofreader.co.uk/

Publisher logo: Vecteezy.com

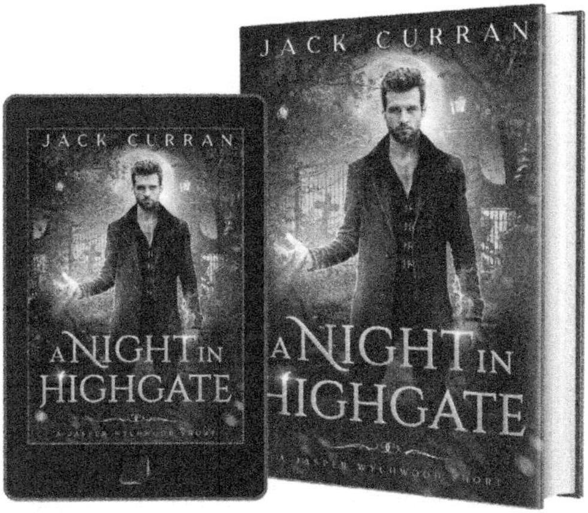

A VICTORIAN GRAVEYARD.

A DEADLY MONSTER.

A NIGHT TO REMEMBER...

Trainee wizard Jasper Wychwood is sent to London's famous Highgate Cemetery to search for a deadly monster. With no backup and no coffee... will he survive the night?

This is a standalone novella that also serves as a great introduction to the Jasper Wychwood Chronicles, an urban fantasy series set in London.

Get your FREE copy at www.jackcurranwrites.com

THE GLASS DAGGER

Swift dressed quickly and was out of his bunk before the tolling of the breakfast bell, before the nightwatchman descended from his lookout above the gatehouse. The castle was quiet—perhaps too quiet. The floorboards groaned as he crept out of his lodging room and into the crisp, early-morning air. Mist was rolling off the mountains, blurring the castle walls and making it difficult to see more than a few paces ahead.

The annual ritual known as the Forging was due to take place in an octagonal building next to the keep called the Furnace. It was normally off-limits to apprentices, but this morning four of them would be permitted to enter. Inside, they would face the culmination of their magical training—a test which would determine their fitness as wizards and representatives of the illustrious Order of Eight. Another group of four apprentices had entered the Furnace the evening before to face the same test. Swift didn't know if any of them had passed the test.

He hugged the shadows, aware that he was fogging the air with each breath. He had a nagging feeling he was being watched. His roughspun tunic chafed his skin and was too thin to offer much protection against the cold. He'd normally have worn a rabbit fur coat and boots lined with sheep's wool, but today he'd dressed in light clothes to maximise his speed and agility.

The archmages would never say what the Forging entailed. Rumours had it the eight apprentices who faced the test each year were spirited away afterwards through the tunnels underneath the castle to begin their postings for the Order.

Whatever happened over the next few hours, Swift's apprenticeship would soon be at an end.

Once he reached the door to the Furnace, he hunkered down and made his body as small as possible. As he waited for the breakfast bell, he studied the long, sweeping wall that marked the eastern boundary of the castle.

Sly gave himself away as he darted across the battlements, his cloak flapping like a bat's wing between the crenelations. Was it carelessness, or craft, that caused him to reveal himself?

Did he want to be seen, to lull Swift into a false sense of safety? Swift covered his mouth with the loose cloth of his tunic to conceal his breath, although he was sure Sly had seen him already.

When the breakfast bell sounded a few minutes later, there was a faint click, and the door swung open of its own accord.

The Furnace contained a single room, lit by a pair of smouldering braziers. Smoke hung heavy in the air. The floor was bare, cold earth, which Swift could feel through his thin shoes. There was some sort of kiln or smithing stove in the centre of the room, connected to a chimney.

'It seems the Furnace is aptly named.'

Swift whirled around. Sly was standing a few feet behind him, smiling. Pleased with himself for sneaking up on Swift unnoticed. Swift cursed silently. He'd need to be sharper than this during the Forging.

'Do you think the archmages are planning to throw us inside that thing?' Sly asked. 'Burn away our impurities?'

'Not all of us,' Swift said. 'But perhaps one or two.'

Sly's laugh turned into a cough. He was a small, wiry young man who had nearly died from consumption as a child—although Swift wasn't supposed to know that. He had a crop of greasy black hair and was dressed in a black shirt, grey breeches, and a faded purple scarf. Apprentices were only permitted to wear plain clothes; anything that smacked of individuality or vanity was strictly prohibited.

When they'd first met, Swift had felt sorry for Sly. He was cursed with a persistent dry cough that sometimes caused him to double over and hack until his face turned bright red. Swift had once asked one of the archmages if a healer could be brought to the castle to help him, but his request was ignored. The archmages only took an interest in the apprentices' health if they seemed at risk of dying.

But Sly didn't need or want pity. He was more than capable of looking out for himself.

'This kiln must have something to do with the Forging,' Sly said, 'or else why would it be here?'

Swift noticed that there was a long pair of metal tongs lying beside the kiln. Before he could give much thought to how they might be used in the Forging, if at all, the door clicked open again.

'Hello, Fierce,' Sly said. 'Glad you could join us. I was worried you were going to be late.'

Fierce strode into the Furnace, glancing first at Swift and Sly, then at the kiln. She was a seven foot tall mountain of rippling muscle with barbarian blood in her veins, if the rumours were to be believed.

Grim—the fourth and final apprentice due to take part in the Forging—was just behind her. He was tall and thin, with hollow cheeks and a nose like a beak. Grim had few friends among the other apprentices, but enjoyed the grudging respect of his peers because of his natural skill with necromantic magic. Sly greeted him, but Grim took no notice and slunk into a corner, muttering something under his breath.

Now that they were all assembled, Swift wondered who would be the greatest threat in whatever task lay ahead.

A few minutes later an elderly woman entered the Furnace. She wore a black, full-length robe beneath a panelled waistcoat decorated with silver thread. She carried a metal staff with claw-like spikes at the end designed to hold a precious stone, although there was no stone there at present.

Swift's nervousness increased. This woman was Ashar, one of the strictest and least forgiving of all the archmages. If she was going to oversee the Forging, they were likely in for a rough morning.

Ashar locked the door behind her and strode towards the kiln. There weren't any windows in the Furnace, Swift realised, and only one door, which was now locked. They were sealed in.

The four apprentices gathered silently around her.

'You have all spent the past eight years learning the ways of our Order, the ways of true magic,' Ashar said. 'You believe this training makes you worthy of representing the Order of Eight in our dealings with the outside world. You are wrong.'

Swift glanced at the other apprentices, who looked as worried as he felt. *What does she mean by that?*

'Your eight years of training were necessary, but not sufficient, to enable you to ascend to full wizardhood. To achieve that, you must succeed in the test known as the Forging.'

'True wizardhood requires not only years of study but also mastery of the most powerful substance known to humankind. A substance which allows our magic to soar to unparalleled heights. I am speaking of *wizard glass*.'

There was a moment of stunned silence as the apprentices absorbed what Ashar had said. Swift tried to remember what he knew of wizard glass. It had featured in a bedtime story his mother had told him once, about a village conjurer who found an orb of wizard glass and used it to extend his life. He lived for two hundred years but eventually went mad and was killed by one of his great-great-grandchildren.

'I thought wizard glass was a myth,' Fierce said. 'Like alchemy, or the chalice of the silent prophet.'

'Our studies didn't include anything about wizard glass,' Swift pointed out.

'Then consider this your final lesson,' Ashar said coldly, as she withdrew something from under the folds of her robe. It was a precious stone that changed colour as it caught the light of the braziers. It was slightly larger than a man's fist and still in a raw, uncut form, as if it had been recently dug out of the earth. Ashar placed the stone into a small crucible that looked like a black cup, which she gripped with the tongs. She placed the crucible carefully inside the kiln, then placed the tongs to one side and began muttering under her breath. Flames flickered to life within the kiln and heat wafted out of it.

Ashar spent the next few minutes working the kiln, eventually bringing out a tray with a glittering piece of glass resting on it. Swift realised the tray was actually a template into which Ashar had poured the molten glass. She carefully placed it on the floor then tipped water from a flask over it. The template sizzled and steamed.

As the steam dissipated, Swift saw Ashar had created a dagger from the raw chunk of wizard glass. It comprised a single piece of shaped glass with a smooth handle and a thin, sharp blade. Had it been made of metal, it might have been a weapon favoured by a thief or a street brawler, but as it was made of wizard glass, it glowed and sparkled with a kaleidoscope of coloured light.

Ashar removed one of the gloves she was wearing and knelt beside the dagger. Her naked hand was extremely pale, as if coated in a skin-tight layer of frost. The dagger hissed and steamed as she picked it up, but Ashar didn't flinch. She was a master of frost—a winter wizard—so had no fear of getting burned. The apprentices watched with wide eyes as the dagger cooled in her hand.

'A dagger is a strange weapon for a wizard,' Fierce mumbled.

The same thought had occurred to Swift as well. *Why make a dagger, of all things?*

'When the Forging is over,' Ashar said, 'one of you may reforge this dagger into a weapon fit for a mage. A wand, or an orb to top a staff, for instance.'

'Only one of us?' Sly asked.

Ashar nodded. 'Only one. At present, the glass is still in its raw form, able to receive power but not project it. A further step is required if the wizard glass is to gain full potency.'

'You're going to kill one of us, aren't you?' Grim said, his eyes round with fear. 'That's what you're talking about. You're going to stab one of us so the glass can absorb our power!'

Ashar's face betrayed no emotion. Her eyes were shining blue pools. 'Alas, one death is not sufficient. This is why we don't speak openly about the Forging. Wizard glass only quickens after it receives the *ethos* of three, fully trained mages.'

Swift felt a chill deep in his bones. *Ethos* was a word common to several human languages. The Order used it to refer to a wizard's magical power, but back in Swift's provincial home it meant a person's immortal spirit, the essence which lives on when their body dies. Swift had never been especially spiritual, but Ashar seemed to be saying that three of them would lose not only their lives but also their *immortal souls*, while only one would survive to become a wizard.

'No wonder you kept this a secret,' Sly said. He normally affected an aloof, mocking tone, but even he couldn't keep the fear and dismay out of his voice.

'This is hard on all of us,' Fierce said. 'We always knew the path to wizardhood would be paved with pain, but we didn't think it would be—'

'—paved with death,' Swift said.

Ashar looked at each of them in turn, her eyes bright and cold as ice. *Why couldn't she sacrifice herself to power the glass?* Swift thought. *At least she's had a chance to properly live before dying.*

'Each of you will have a fair chance,' Ashar said. 'Shortly, I will place the dagger somewhere within the tunnels underneath the Furnace for you to find.'

'You mean we have to find it, then use it to kill the others?'

'Precisely.'

Swift looked at his fellow apprentices. They looked stunned. Would they accept these terms and take their chances? What if they all refused to cooperate?

Swift had expected the Forging to be difficult. Training with the Order of Eight had been gruelling from start to finish; many would-be apprentices had dropped out over the years. But he hadn't expected the culmination of his training to be a gladiatorial fight to the death. Was that what being a wizard came down to? Murdering your rivals? The spoils of victory going to whoever spilled the most blood?

Fierce muttered something under her breath.

Sly stared at the glass dagger with wide, greedy eyes.

A muscle in Grim's jaw twitched. He backed away from the dagger.

'This isn't what I signed up for,' he said. 'My father is a sergeant in the Duke or Onteel's expeditionary force. He won't stand for this! He'll come looking for me if I stop writing to him.'

'You haven't written to him in six years,' Ashar said evenly. 'Don't pretend to have forgotten the agreement you made when you began your apprenticeship. You gave up your name, your sex, your familial connections, your friends, your loyalty to lord and land. The man you were no longer exists. The same goes for all of you.'

Grim had once told Swift his birth name, but Swift couldn't remember what it was. Severe punishments were meted out for using birth names, or for talking about their old lives. Despite this, for the first year of his apprenticeship Swift had said a prayer each night for the health of his mother and brother. But eventually he stopped as their faces faded from his memory.

‘I don’t remember agreeing to give up my life, never mind my soul,’ Grim said, moving towards the door. ‘I won’t make any trouble, I swear. I’ll leave the castle quietly and will never speak of the Order or the Forging for as long as I live. You have my word, archmage.’

Ashar studied his face. ‘If you leave now, that will mean giving up on becoming a wizard forever. You will never be allowed to dabble in magic.’

‘I understand. I’ll forsake magic forever, if you’ll allow me to leave.’

Ashar seemed to give his request serious consideration. Would she accept it? What if all four of them asked to be released from the Forging? Was that allowed?

‘Very well,’ she said at last. ‘Come here—you’ll need to use my key to leave the Furnace.’

Grim looked mightily relieved. He avoided the eyes of his fellow apprentices as he moved back towards Ashar, who was pawing at her coat, presumably looking for the key. Then, without warning, she struck out at Grim. The movement was so quick that Swift didn’t at first understand what had happened, but then Grim doubled over and Swift saw the glass dagger protruding from his stomach.

Grim opened his mouth to scream, but could only manage a dry, rasping sound. Terror contorted his face. His skin turned pale and seemed to shrink, clinging tightly to his jaw and cheekbones. He stared in horror at his hands, which now looked like those of an old man. His eyes turned milky white, as if afflicted by cataracts. He sank to the floor. His breath became laboured and then stopped altogether.

Ashar waited for him to stop moving, then knelt down and yanked the dagger out of his gut. Curiously, there was no blood, only a dark wound like a bruise beneath Grim's ripped shirt. The dagger glittered in Ashar's hand and appeared to be clean.

'The rules of the Forging have stood for centuries and cannot be negotiated,' Ashar said sternly. 'This is how we have inducted new members into our Order for centuries, ever since the original eight founders first learned the secrets of wizard glass. Now that you have entered the Furnace, you must complete the Forging. There are only two outcomes available to you now: wizardhood, or death.'

'I WILL ENTER THE tunnels ahead of you,' Ashar said. It would have been impossible to tell by her tone or demeanour that she'd drained the life from a young man moments earlier. 'Once I have hidden the dagger, you will enter the tunnels one at a time to search for it. You must kill your rivals using the glass dagger, and not by any other means. Other than that, you may use any tactics to succeed.'

She ushered them forward, and they obediently gathered around her. *Like little lambs to the slaughter*, Swift thought bleakly.

Ashar reached into her coat and brought out four brass keys. The shaft of each key ended in a symbol that matched the four suits in a pack of playing cards: the Harvest Sun, the Bleeding Heart, the Roving Eye, and the Crescent Moon. Ashar briefly turned her back on the apprentices, then offered the four keys with the teeth pointing upwards, so that the suit symbols were hidden behind her fists.

'Choose your key. You first, Swift.'

Swift chose the key on the far left, but instantly regretted his choice. It was the Crescent Moon, which was considered to be the weakest suit in most card games.

Behind him, Sly laughed. 'Perhaps that's only fair,' he said. 'Fierce and I are slouches compared with you. I'm sure you'll catch up.'

Perhaps I will, Swift thought, *but maybe not before one of you has found the glass dagger.*

'You'll enter the tunnels last,' Ashar confirmed. 'Fierce, you next.'

Fierce picked the Bleeding Heart, and then Sly selected the Harvest Sun, which meant that he would go first and Fierce second.

'Three bells will ring in succession to tell you when to enter the tunnels.' Ashar smiled thinly. 'I'll see one of you later.'

Just one, Swift thought. *Because the others will be dead.*

The tunnels were apparently accessed through a trap-door next to the kiln. Ashar used a key of her own to open it and disappear inside.

As soon as Ashar was gone, Sly scurried over to Fierce and began a whispered conversation. Swift felt sick with nerves. *Why does it seem like everything is going against me before I've even entered the tunnels?*

When the pair eventually drew apart, Sly's eyes were glowing with satisfaction.

'We've swapped keys,' he announced. 'Fierce is going to use the Harvest Sun key to enter the tunnels first, then I will follow with the Bleeding Heart key. She is slower than either of us, so it seems only fair that she should get a head start.'

'I didn't know you were such a stickler for fairness,' Swift said dryly.

Sly shrugged. 'There is much you do not know about me.'

His words were probably meant to sound dignified, but he couldn't prevent a smug smile from appearing on his lips. Swapping keys with Fierce had nothing to do with fairness, and they all knew it. This was a fight to the death. All their lives were on the line. Sly wasn't interested in a fair fight, he was interested in winning. In surviving. He and Fierce had struck some sort of deal. Perhaps they'd agreed to cooperate to kill Swift before turning on each other. It would only be a temporary alliance, but it would increase both their odds of being the sole survivor when all was said and done.

Increase their odds—and decrease Swift's to almost nothing.

How could he possibly win against both of them?

A short while later, they heard a bell tolling somewhere in the rafters of the Furnace. Fierce didn't waste any time—she thrust the Sun key into the lock in the trap door and leapt into the tunnels. The door banged shut behind her.

'I had no choice but to make a deal with Fierce,' Sly said, leaning against the kiln. 'She's the best fighter of the three of us—a born battle mage.'

'Whatever deal you've made won't stop her killing you when she's done with me,' Swift observed.

'I agree. That's why you and I should make our own agreement.'

Swift laughed out loud, a braying laugh which may have sounded a touch unhinged.'Only you would have the gall to offer an alliance to both your rivals. I'll take my chances alone, thank you.'

'Suit yourself.'

Swift mentally shook himself. Sly was trying to get inside his head, trying to confuse and unbalance him. He needed to ignore these mind games and focus on his own skills, his own ability to survive.

The bell tolled a second time. Sly approached the trap door.

'Good luck, my friend,' he said. 'Consider my offer.'

Sly entered the tunnels and Swift was left alone in the Furnace. The enormity of the task in front of him threatened to overwhelm him. He clasped his hands together to stop them shaking and tried not to look at Grim's broken body.

He waited beside the trapdoor and entered the tunnels the moment the bell tolled for the third time. Once the door shut behind him, the darkness was total. Panic seized his chest. He'd expected there to be at least some light down here, but there was none. How was he supposed to find the dagger if he couldn't see?

The tunnels smelled of dirt and damp. Swift felt his way forward with his hands, moving with agonising slowness. The ground was rough and hard and covered with stones of various sizes, some smooth and round, others sharp as knives. He tripped several times and sliced his hand within minutes of going through the trapdoor.

He wondered if the archmages were laughing at him.

Eventually, he spied a pinprick of light ahead. He increased his speed and reached a small room with wooden boards braced against the walls and held in place by metal rings. Three of the rings also held torches that burned with magelight. There was a fourth ring lined up next to the other three, but this one was empty.

The torches were not here by chance. Ashar probably lit them on her way to hide the glass dagger. Swift went to pick up the nearest torch, then hesitated. There were three torches left out of four, which meant that either Fierce or Sly had taken a torch, but the other hadn't. Why not?

Perhaps because holding a torch in such a dark place was like painting a luminous target on your back. He guessed it was Sly, arriving second, who had foreseen this potential risk and decided to make do without a torch.

Swift felt torn. Without a torch, he'd have to shuffle forward like a blind man. With it, he left himself wide open to a sneak attack. What should he do? His training had taught him not to make rash decisions. Plan your strategy in advance, then execute it. Be flexible, but don't accept every offer of help. Blessings are sometimes curses in disguise.

He needed to work out his tactics. He needed a plan that played to his strengths.

When they'd first arrived at the castle, the apprentices were told that they must discard their old names and everything that went with them. Family, land, nation. Even sex. For the first few weeks, the new apprentices were nameless, until eventually they were given new names by the archmages.

By the end of his first month at the castle, Sly had played several tricks on the other apprentices, and persuaded one of them to steal him extra rations from the kitchen.

Fierce had started three fights and won them all.

Grim complained about everything from the moment he arrived. The food, the bedding, the castle, the archmages, the other apprentices. What was the point of practising spells all day, when they were all doomed to fail?

Swift, unlike the others, liked his new name. It described him perfectly. As a child, he'd earned money as a courier, dashing between the local villages and farms to deliver letters. He'd enjoyed running across fields and along muddy paths dotted with puddles. Speed had always been his strength. During his studies with the Order of Eight, he'd opted to pay particular attention to the methods of the legendary mage assassins, men and women who'd used magic to kill quickly and silently.

One particular spell came to mind now. He'd never actually tried it before, although he knew how it was supposed to work. It was extremely dangerous, but it might provide a solution to his current dilemma.

He placed his right hand in the centre of the nearest torch-flame. Gritting his teeth against the pain, he willed the magelight to take root on the back of his hand. Once it had, he braced himself, then brought the magelight into contact with his right eye.

The pain was like nothing he'd felt before. Immense and overwhelming. But he didn't stop. After a few agonising seconds, he moved his flaming hand to his other eye. The pain surged through him as both his eyes blazed and shed tears at the same time.

When the magelight finally fizzled out, Swift stumbled backwards and fell to the ground, moaning with pain, wondering if he would ever see properly again. Eventually, and with trepidation, he opened his eyes again and stood up, leaning on the tunnel wall for support. His eyes were sore, watering and blurry—but they worked, better than before. The tunnels now appeared to be bathed in purplish light. Although everything looked strange, he could see into all the dark corners even without a source of light. He walked away from the torches to be sure the effect still worked in a completely dark area. To his relief, it did.

One of the side effects of this spell, he remembered, was that his eyes would now glow, which meant Fierce and Sly might see him coming. It wasn't ideal, but at least he could shut his eyes to conceal himself if he really needed to.

However, there was another problem: he'd lost most of his peripheral vision. The edges of his sight were completely dark, and there were black spots floating through the centre of his vision too.

Was this damage permanent? Would it get worse?

He told himself it didn't matter, and tried to focus on his only goal: survival.

Navigating the tunnels was still difficult. Most of them were only about five feet across and in places the ceiling was low enough that he had to crouch to make it through. He came to several forks and junctions in the tunnels, and chose his route forward more-or-less at random. He encountered no signs or landmarks of any kind. For all he knew, he was walking in a circle. He started to wonder if the real danger wasn't being killed by Fierce or Sly, but getting permanently lost in this wretched place.

He realised after a while that there were bones among the rocks and other detritus that littered the ground. There were even a few skeletons, complete with skulls. He shuddered with fear and revulsion. Were these the remains of apprentices who had died during previous Forgings?

As he pondered this, his foot snagged on something and he almost fell face first into the ground. Once he'd steadied himself, he saw that he'd tripped on a body. Not a skeleton—a corpse, fully clothed. There was a nasty, black wound on its chest, above the heart, much like the fatal wound Grim had sustained earlier. It looked as though the flesh, fat and sinew had been sucked out of the body, leaving behind grey, dried-out skin clinging to the bones like thin cloth.

Swift's heart beat faster as he recognised the clothing. Chain mail under a wine-coloured tabard, a belt buckle decorated with the image of a stag. This was the body of Proud, the son of a knight from the western dukedom, who had been part of the Forging that took part last night. Not that Swift was supposed to know that Proud's father was a knight, but, despite the archmages' rules, sometimes apprentices did exchange information about their families and former lives. Proud had been the closest thing to a friend that Swift had had during his training. He turned away from the body as a wave of grief passed through him. He couldn't afford to let sadness overtake him, but it was hard seeing that his friend had meant such a cruel end.

Proud had obviously been killed with the glass dagger—or rather, a different glass dagger that had been forged last night. Which meant that one of the other three apprentices from last night's Forging had won the contest and become a wizard.

A frightening thought occurred to Swift: what if only one apprentice from *both groups combined* was permitted to attain wizardhood? What if last night's winner was still down here with his or her own glass dagger, waiting to kill Swift and the rest of his group to be crowned overall winner of this year's Forging? If true, it would mean Ashar had lied, or told them a half-truth, but that would hardly be surprising. The archmages weren't above telling outright lies if it suited them.

Ashar had said that it took the deaths of *three* apprentices to quicken wizard glass, but what if it actually took *seven*?

EVENTUALLY, SWIFT ENTERED A large, open chamber. It was a relief to finally be out of the narrow twisting tunnels. He took a deep, slow breath and looked around. The chamber was filled with some kind of crystalline substance that was jutting out of the floor and walls. Swift approached one particularly large crystal spike to examine it more closely. It seemed to change colour as he looked at it, from green to blue to indigo to crimson red.

It was wizard glass, he realised. Raw wizard glass.

The Furnace—and the whole castle—was built on a huge deposit of wizard glass! This was probably why the Order of Eight founded their settlement here. The stories that Swift had heard about wizard glass suggested it was vanishingly rare. If so, this might represent the largest deposit in the world.

There was probably enough glass in this room alone to outfit every mage on the continent with an armoury of magical weapons. But mining the glass wasn't the problem—drenching it in the blood of several fully trained apprentices was obviously the bottleneck that prevented it from being exploited on an industrial scale.

Swift wandered between the huge spikes of wizard glass, keeping his eyes peeled for any sign of movement. Due to the glow emanating from the spikes, it was much easier to see here than it had been in the tunnels, but there were still plenty of dark corners where Sly or Fierce might be hiding.

He soon found another relatively fresh corpse propped against a spike of glass. This body had the same characteristic black wound and grey, wizened skin. As before, it didn't take Swift long to deduce who the body might have belonged to, for Sly's purple scarf was tied around its neck.

Swift had never liked Sly, but a wave of sadness enveloped him nonetheless. Sly had earned his name, and was a difficult person to like, but did he really deserve this?

Swift didn't have long to wallow in his feelings. A new source of light brightened the dim chamber, causing the spikes of wizard glass to sparkle and shimmer. Swift whirled around and saw a tall figure entering the chamber on the far side carrying a magelight torch. He put his hand up to partially shield his eyes—with his newly sensitised eyes, the torchlight almost blinded him. Through his fingers he saw the figure was carrying an axe in their other hand. The weapon seemed to be outlined with flickering stripes of coloured light, which meant it was a conjured axe—a weapon created by magic.

Unfortunately, there was no opportunity to hide. Fierce was already staring right at Swift.

'Hello. Fancy meeting you here.'

Fierce strode forward, betraying no fear or anxiety.

Of course not. She was always the bravest of all of us.

As Fierce got closer and Swift's eyes adjusted to the new condition of light, he saw her more clearly. Her tunic—which had been in perfect condition earlier—was torn in several places.

Is that from fighting Sly? Did she kill him, then lie in wait near his body?

'Greetings, Swift,' Fierce said. 'Under different circumstances, I would offer to accept your surrender. Give you a quick and easy death.'

'I don't think the glass dagger allows for easy deaths,' Swift said. He wondered if Sly's death had been just as agonising as Grim's.

'True enough. Before we fight, I wish to say that I respect your skills and your tenacity.'

Swift suppressed a laugh. Fierce sounded less like a barbarian or a battle mage, and more like a chivalric knight from a bedtime story.

'Err, thank you,' he said. 'I respect you too.'

Fierce nodded. 'But from now on, I will show you no respect and give no quarter.'

'Fair enough. But before we fight, could you tell me what happened to Sly. Did you—'

But Fierce was done talking. She roared, then lifted the conjured axe up to her ear and threw it. It tumbled through the air sparkling with light like a firework. Swift dived out of the way just in time, and the axe whistled past his head.

Fierce continued roaring while she charged, holding the blazing torch in front of her. The bright light dazzled Swift, who dropped to the floor and scrambled behind the nearest chunk of wizard glass. Fierce rounded the spike and aimed a kick at Swift. She probably meant to kick him in the stomach, but he was turning away so she caught him in the kidneys instead.

Gritting his teeth against the pain, Swift dragged himself to his feet and ran away. To his relief, he saw that Fierce wasn't pursuing him. Instead, she'd gone to fetch her axe from where it had fallen. He needed to use these few seconds wisely. If he tried to go toe-to-toe with Fierce, he'd be dead within minutes. He needed a better strategy.

In the accounts he'd read of the great assassin mages, it was said that they sometimes walked calmly into the middle of a room full of enemies, sat down on the floor, and closed their eyes. Suicidal as it might sound, Swift's apprenticeship had taught him that there had been method to their madness.

Though his heart was beating fast and every sinew of his body screamed at him to flee, Swift mastered his fear and sat cross legged on the ground between two jutting spikes of wizard glass, making no effort to conceal himself. As he closed his eyes, he glimpsed Fierce staring at him with her axe in hand. Sweat dribbled from his forehead onto his eyelids. He felt himself trembling, but resolved not to let fear control his actions. He'd practised this spell many times before, although never with the looming threat of death hanging over him.

He first slowed his breathing, then stopped breathing altogether. He listened to the pounding of his own heart, until the beating slowed and stopped as well. His fingers and toes went numb, then his whole body disconnected from his mind. His head lolled forward and his shoulders slumped. He reached out with his concentration, and *felt*, rather than saw, Fierce stomping towards him. She moved slowly, like a clumsy giant wading through a swamp.

Swift opened his eyes. Fierce was staring at him with a puzzled look on her face.

Thank the gods we had different tutors, otherwise she might've understood what I'm doing.

Swift stood up, but Fierce's eyes remained fixed on his previous location. She was in the process of raising her axe to strike, but was doing so at a snail's pace. Swift, by contrast, felt light and nimble. From Fierce's perspective, the spell would only last a couple of seconds, but within that brief span Swift would be able to move much faster than her and do a lot of damage.

He sidestepped Fierce and reached into his boot to retrieve a small blade. It wasn't much bigger than a paring knife, but it would have to do. Fierce's expression told Swift she now had some inkling of what was happening, but she was too slow to do anything about it. Swift stepped behind her and slashed her leg just above the ankle. He moved to strike her other leg, but as he did so, the spell lost its power and Fierce spun around. As time returned to its normal flow, Fierce tried to swing her axe but lost balance because of her injured leg. She stumbled forward and nearly fell on top of Swift.

Fierce kept hold of her conjured axe, but she dropped the torch. Swift quickly stamped out the flame, plunging them both into darkness, handing himself an advantage. With his inflamed eyes, he could still see reasonably well, while Fierce would be as good as blind.

Fierce backed away, clearly stunned and wondering what to do. Even blinded and injured, she was still a formidable foe. Swift still didn't have the glass dagger, so for now he needed to escape this fight.

He sprinted back the way he'd come, but the fight had disorientated him, and he soon found himself in an unfamiliar corner of the chamber, with only a glowing chunk of wizard glass in front of him and no escape route in sight. He heard Fierce charging up behind him and turned around. She'd transformed her axe into a war hammer that had a longer reach than the axe. A clever move. She could swing it in a wide arc and have a decent chance of hitting him, even in the dark. And as long as his eyes were open, she'd be able to see roughly where he was.

Fierce swung the war hammer. Swift clamped his eyes shut and dropped to the floor, his heart in his mouth. He felt a whoosh of air as the war hammer cleaved the space above his head. There was a loud clunk as the weapon struck something hard. He opened his eyes and saw that the war hammer was buried in a chunk of wizard glass. Fierce tried to pull it out, but it was buried deep. A single, jagged piece of glass had been chipped off the larger spike and now lay on the floor.

With Fierce still straining to retrieve her war hammer, Swift grabbed the shard of wizard glass and thrust it into her stomach. She released her hold on the war hammer and stared down at her wound. Swift stepped in close, pulled the glass shard out of her stomach and thrust it into her neck. As before, there was no blood, but the skin of Fierce's neck turned black as if stained with ink. She tried to say something, but she could only make a wheezing noise. Her flesh seemed to dissolve and her body shrivelled; her skin clung to her bones like cheap paper. She collapsed onto the ground and stopped moving.

The jagged slice of wizard glass sparkled in Swift's hand, bursting with multicoloured light. It wasn't the glass dagger Ashar had forged, but it had absorbed Fierce's *ethos* anyway.

Swift was shaking. He'd studied the art of killing, but had never taken a life before. He told himself he hadn't decided on the rules of the Forging. None of this was his idea. If he hadn't killed Fierce, she'd certainly have killed him. He'd had no choice.

After some searching around, he found an exit to the chamber which was different from the one he'd entered by. He left and took the glass shard with him.

Was he supposed to feel elated, he wondered? He'd won. Fierce, Sly and Grim were all dead, but his victory tasted bitter, and might turn out to be hollow. Would Ashar and the other archmages agree that he had won the Forging? He hadn't killed Sly, and he'd slain Fierce with a random shard of wizard glass, not with the glass dagger. Would they care? Would they punish him for straying outside the rules?

He decided his best chance lay in finding the glass dagger and taking it, along with the broken shard containing Fierce's *ethos*, to Ashar. He'd explain what had happened and hope she would accept his victory. Surely, she could blend the two pieces of glass together in the kiln?

Swift had been eager to get away from Fierce's body as quickly as possible, but now he hurried back to it. He hurriedly searched her corpse, avoiding looking at her face. Like him, she had a couple of knives hidden in her clothes, but there was no sign of the glass dagger. Although he hated himself for rifling her body, he forced himself to check carefully to be absolutely certain.

After several minutes searching, he was forced to conclude that Fierce simply didn't have the dagger. Did that mean she'd killed Sly with a random shard of wizard glass? Or had she found the glass dagger, killed Sly with it, then lost it again?

Both scenarios were possible, but neither seemed likely.

Swift's head was throbbing with a headache. Black shapes were swimming across his vision. The pain was unpleasant but bearable. Worse was the growing fear that his eyesight might be permanently damaged. The seeing-spell was dangerous and meant to be used in short bursts only.

He found Fierce's torch on the ground and lit it. Once he'd removed the magelight from his eyes, he saw that there were persistent dark spots floating across the centre of his sight, while some of his peripheral vision was gone entirely. He told himself that it was a price worth paying to survive and achieve wizardhood and entry into the Order of Eight, but deep down he was distraught. Even if he was accepted into the Order, there was no guarantee this damage could be repaired.

Regardless, he pressed on through winding tunnels and various chambers containing crumbling and rusty mining equipment. It appeared the Order had given up mining wizard glass, probably because it had little value unless quickened by the *ethos* of apprentices. At best it could be turned into jewellery and other trinkets which could be sold for a modest profit, but doing so would reveal to the world that the Order was sitting on a vast horde of wizard glass, a substance many believed to be mythical. No doubt the archmages preferred to keep their stock of wizard glass a secret.

He came eventually to a narrow shaft with a ladder leading down. At the bottom was a junction with three diverging tunnels. At first glance they looked identical, but when he carefully inspected each with his torch, he found a small piece of dull grey metal on the ground a few feet inside one of the tunnels. The metal was in the shape of a number eight or, if viewed sideways, an infinity symbol—the symbol of the Order of Eight. There was a pin and hinge on the back, which meant this was almost certainly the clasp for a cloak.

Had this clasp dropped here by chance, or was it left here intentionally to mark the correct path forward—the path that led to the glass dagger?

Swift left the clasp where it was and proceeded down the tunnel. He soon came to a large chamber containing a narrow stone bridge crossing a wide chasm. The bridge led to a flat area on the other side with a statue of a wizard brandishing a staff.

There was a large chest at the feet of the statue, lit by a small magelight torch positioned just above it. The air was cool down here, and there was a gentle breeze. Swift peered over the edge of the stone bridge. It was very dark. He searched on the ground and found a stone to drop over the side. A few seconds later, the stone plopped loudly into a body of water at the bottom of the chasm.

Swift knew he was being watched. He wasn't sure how he knew, but he was certain of it. He'd been led to this place on purpose, and now his approach was being closely observed. He replayed the events of the past couple of hours in his mind: from stumbling on Sly's body and fighting Fierce, to finding a metal clasp which conveniently pointed the way forward.

He cleared his throat, then said, 'Show yourself Sly. I've had enough of your games.'

He held up his torch and fed magical power into it, causing the flame to flare brightly. Light bloomed throughout the chamber.

A cloaked figure was revealed lying in the middle of the bridge. The figure stood up and scowled at Swift, the glass dagger glittering in his hand.

'How did you know I was here?' Sly asked. 'I hoped you'd find my body in the glass chamber, but perhaps you overlooked it?'

'I saw it,' Swift said. 'But it is difficult to tell one corpse from another when they've been slain by the glass dagger. I found a corpse wearing your purple scarf, but that wasn't conclusive. You might have wrapped your scarf around any mouldering old corpse to lull your opponents into thinking you were dead.'

Sly smiled thinly. 'It worked on Fierce.'

'It almost worked on me too, but then Fierce attacked me using a conjured axe. There was no sign of the glass dagger when I searched her body afterwards, so I guessed she hadn't killed you after all. Which meant you were still alive.'

'Very logical.'

'I wasn't absolutely certain until I saw that you'd left behind your metal clasp to mark the way forward. That made it obvious I was being led into a trap.'

Sly shrugged. 'It wasn't subtle, I admit, but I had to ensure you came this way, otherwise we might both have wandered blindly around these tunnels for weeks without finding each other.'

Sly's tone was casual, and Swift supposed he still had good reason to feel confident. He had the glass dagger in his hand, after all.

'So it comes down to you or me. One lives and becomes a wizard, while the other dies.'

'Not necessarily,' Sly said. 'I'd like to make you an offer.'

Swift smiled ruefully. If Sly was the last human alive, he'd try to strike a deal with the trees and the mountains. 'Are you going to offer to kill me quickly?'

Sly shook his head. 'I know what you're thinking—there can be no more deals when there are only two of us left and one dagger. But I believe there is a third contestant in our nasty little game.'

'Fierce is dead.'

'Not Fierce. I've been carefully checking all the corpses I've encountered, looking in particular for the bodies of the apprentices who came here last night. I located the bodies of Cruel, Fickle, and Pale—but not Proud. I watched them all enter the Furnace last night, so I know what they were wearing. I believe Proud is still alive and is waiting for a chance to strike down the last survivor of our group so he can take the glass dagger for himself.'

Swift frowned. 'But if he survived last night's Forging, he'll have a glass dagger of his own, won't he? Ashar will have let him leave the tunnels.'

Sly spat over the side of the bridge. 'Don't be naïve. Ashar said one of our group of four would ascend to wizardhood, but don't you think it's more likely to be *one of eight*? The ultimate survivor from both groups?'

Swift felt a sinking feeling in his gut. There was no way to be certain—Sly was only guessing—but his instincts told him the theory was probably correct. The Order of Eight was built around that magical number. The eight archmages were obsessed by it.

'Let's say you're right. What are you proposing?'

Sly took a few tentative steps forward. 'That we team up, temporarily. Hunt down Proud. If we instead fight each other now, the victor will most likely be injured—and will be easy prey for Proud. But if we work together, we can both increase our odds for success.'

It almost made sense. Almost. But Swift had seen Proud's body earlier and knew that he was dead, so the theory was wrong.

It was in Sly's nature to wheel and deal, even when deals and schemes seemed impossible, but this offer was surely nothing more than a ruse to get Swift to lower his guard. A last attempt to avoid facing his last opponent in a fair fight. A fight which, in any case, favoured him, since he already possessed the glass dagger.

But Swift had an advantage of his own, one Sly knew nothing of.

'Very well. We'll work together, at least until Proud is dead.' He strode across the stone bridge, trying to appear confident. 'Do you have any idea where he is? Is this chamber a dead end, or do the tunnels continue beyond this statue?'

Sly was staring at him with narrowed eyes, clearly trying to decide whether his acquiescence was genuine. 'The tunnels loop back on themselves,' he said. 'If you look behind the statue—'

Swift whipped the glass shard out of his pocket and flung it at Sly, who tried to lurch out of the way, but was not quick enough. Swift had spent long hours practising throwing knives, both corporeal and conjured, into a target in a field outside the castle, so his aim was true. The shard punctured Sly's shoulder, then slipped out and dropped onto the bridge.

Sly screamed and staggered backwards. He ripped open the shoulder of his tunic and peered down at the wound. Swift held up the torch so he could see as well. A bruise had appeared on Sly's shoulder and was spreading out rapidly from the point where the shard had struck.

Sly turned and stumbled towards the wizard statue and sat down heavily on the chest underneath it, breathing hard. Swift followed him cautiously, leaving a space between them. The glass dagger was still in Sly's hand, but he seemed too overwhelmed with pain to do anything with it. Would the wound be fatal? Under normal circumstances it wouldn't have been especially serious—a flesh wound—but the dark magic that suffused wizard glass made even a glancing blow potentially fatal.

'Was that... another dagger?' Sly asked between wheezing breaths.

'It was a raw shard of wizard glass that chipped off one of the large spikes during my fight with Fierce.'

'I see. A perfect secret weapon.'

Although he was still gripping the glass dagger, Sly made no hostile moves as Swift drew near.

'Good luck against Proud. He must be a better fighter than I thought if he overcame the other three last night.'

Sly spoke as if his death was inevitable. And perhaps it was.

'Proud's dead,' Swift said. 'I saw his body a couple of hours ago.'

Sly furrowed his brow. 'Are you sure? But that must mean…' He trailed off, his expression growing darker. 'That means there is no hope,' he whispered. 'For either of us.'

Sly raised the dagger and Swift bent his knees, preparing to leap out of the way, but he needn't have bothered. Sly pushed the glass dagger into his own neck and neatly snipped his artery. Blood should have gushed out his neck, but it didn't. It was as if the dagger's magic instantly sealed the wound and clotted the blood.

The light in his eyes faded quickly as his body shrunk. His hand fell open and the glass dagger fell to the ground.

SWIFT LAY DOWN ON the bridge and remained there for some time. The smooth stone felt pleasantly cool and solid through his thin shirt and trousers. He felt strangely calm and disconnected from the horrors he had seen and participated in.

Was he responsible for Sly's death? What about Fierce? What about Grim?

He supposed it didn't matter. The archmages had decided their fates long ago.

He'd survived the Forging but was in no mood to celebrate. Seven doomed apprentices—four last night, three this morning. All dead. Four young people separated from their families, filled up with magic training, then sent to their deaths like lambs to the slaughter. What made Swift so special that he should survive when Sly, Fierce, and the rest had all perished?

Not only did he feel bad about the deaths of his opponents, but, since he'd used a random shard of wizard glass to slay them rather than the glass dagger, he was far from certain that Ashar would accept his victory as legitimate. Perhaps he would suffer the same fate after all.

After his thoughts had circled round and round several times, he finally hauled himself upright. He still felt numb. He took the glass dagger and the glass shard with him and began retracing his steps. At first he thought he might easily get lost and never escape these wretched tunnels, but at the first intersection the glass dagger pulsed warmly in his pocket, nudging him in the right direction. It did the same thing at each junction in the tunnels, guiding him where he needed to go.

About an hour later, he re-emerged from the trapdoor into the Furnace. Ashar was waiting for him, warming her hands in front of the still-smouldering kiln.

'Welcome back, Swift. Congratulations.'

She spoke like a school teacher congratulating her pet pupil. Swift felt disgusted—with Ashar and with himself. Was she going to act as if they weren't both drowning in blood? As if they weren't both murderers?

Ashar must have seen something of Swift's thoughts in his expression, because her smile quickly faded and she looked away from him. Staring into the glowing kiln, she said, 'It is now time to forge a weapon fit for a wizard. What is your choice?'

'My choice?'

'What shall I reforge the glass into?'

Swift shrugged. The question held no interest for him anymore. If he wanted to be a mage assassin, as had always been his intention, there was no need to change the glass dagger from its current form, but he sensed Ashar would disapprove if he asked for that. A dagger was hardly a fit weapon for a mage. So instead he asked for a glass wand.

Ashar nodded, then quickly took the glass dagger and placed it into the crucible, which she fed into the kiln. The kiln hissed and pulsed with heat, but Swift didn't pay close attention to Ashar's work. He felt disinterested in the entire process. He sat on the floor, hugging his knees to his chest.

A while later, Ashar brought the finished piece out of the kiln. She was sweating with the heat and effort but looked pleased with her work.

Swift saw she was holding a glowing sphere of glass—an orb, not a wand. She placed the orb into the space between the spikes protruding from the top of her metal staff. It fit perfectly. Ashar admired her own handiwork, spinning the staff around to view the orb from all angles, seeming in no hurry to explain herself.

As she did this, her body changed. The deep lines on her face disappeared, as did the bulging blue veins on the backs of her hands. Her stringy, white hair thickened and turned a lustrous blonde. Within a few moments, she was a young woman, at least forty years younger than before, in appearance at least.

'You never had any intention of giving the wizard glass to an apprentice, did you? You just needed us to die to power it up. You told us the lives of three trained apprentices were needed, but the truth is it takes four. Or is it eight?'

Ashar was still admiring her prize.. 'The more the better, but we've found eight to be a good number. More than that and the additional benefits diminish.'

She sounds like a moneylender tallying figures, Swift thought.

'So this was all a charade? The Forging was just a trick?'

'Correct. A brutal charade, I admit, but we live in a brutal world. Ultimate power requires ultimate sacrifice.'

'Our sacrifice. Not yours.'

Ashar shrugged. 'That is the way of things.'

'What if your own archmage had done the same thing? What if he had never given way to you?'

'I've never allowed myself to be controlled by another mage,' Ashar sneered. 'You think I'm subverting the Forging, but this is how it has always been.'

'The Order of Eight was founded by eight powerful mages centuries ago. Since then, the world believes that those great mages died and have been replaced by younger men and women in the natural way. But the world is misinformed.'

Swift could already see where this was going. His numbness finally went away, replaced by a burning anger.

All those bodies laying in the tunnels. All those young lives sacrificed. All for nothing.

'I see you understand at last,' Ashar said. 'I and my fellow archmages are not descendents of the original eight founders—*we are the founders*. We've regenerated ourselves countless times through the sacrifice of poor, foolish apprentices like you and your little friends.'

Swift wanted to kick himself. Why hadn't he guessed something like this was going on? Ashar was right to call him foolish. Why had he swallowed the archmages' lies so easily? Why had he trusted them? The archmages had shown themselves to be utterly ruthless and selfish from the start, but, like all the other apprentices, he'd put his misgivings aside in pursuit of power that now proved illusory.

Swift shivered. The Furnace, which had grown warm with the heat of the kiln, now felt icy cold. The orb atop Ashar's staff had turned frosty and white, and the same enchanted frost was creeping down the length of the staff, causing the temperature in the room to plummet. Swift's breath produced puffs of icy fog. Ashar, of course, was immune to the effect.

She's not going to give me a dignified death. I'll die like a lost rabbit perishing in winter's frost.

Swift fumbled towards the kiln, but the warmth coming from it was nowhere near enough to overpower Ashar's spell.

'There is no hope for you, young man,' Ashar said calmly. 'Die in peace, knowing that your *ethos* will be put to good use.'

More like bad *use*, Swift thought bitterly. Ashar's patronising tone helped galvanise him and focus his thoughts. He wasn't ready to embrace death just yet.

'Will you at least grant me a better end than this?' he said. 'I don't want to freeze to death. I think I've earned that much with my efforts in the Forging.'

Ashar tipped her head to the side, apparently considering his argument. 'Perhaps you have,' she agreed.

She approached with her staff pointing at Swift's head. When she was close, he reached into the kiln, grabbed a handful of hot ashes, and threw them into her face with as much force as he could muster. The archmage screamed. She tried to back away but tripped on something on the ground—the tongs she'd used to feed the crucible into the kiln. Swift grabbed the tongs and swung hard. The blow connected with Ashar's temple, sending out a spray of blood and swiftly felling the archmage.

It was a brutal attack that would have killed a burly warrior. But Ashar was still alive.

Swift stared down at the archmage. There was a nasty gash where the tongs had struck, but it was healing rapidly. A layer of frost had appeared over the wound. When it melted a few seconds later, the skin underneath was smooth and uninjured.

'You could strike me like that a thousand times and still not kill me,' Ashar said mildly, confident in her invincibility. But her expression changed when Swift knelt on her stomach, the shard of wizard glass in his hand. She lunged for her staff, but Swift used his weight to pin her to the floor, then stabbed her in the neck. Once, twice, three times. Then he plunged the shard into her chest, where her heart was, assuming she had one.

After that, things went hazy. He kept on stabbing her, long after she stopped moving. The glass shard twinkled more brightly than ever.

With his rage satisfied—for the time being at least—Swift prepared to leave. He didn't want to lug around an unwieldy staff, so he ripped out the glass orb and pocketed it. The door to the Furnace was locked, but Swift had studied lock picking and made quick work of the simple bolt lock. Outside, the sun was setting. He slipped out of the castle quickly and silently, using the entrance usually reserved for visiting tradespeople. A pair of startled, first year apprentices noticed him leaving but didn't intervene. Fortunately, he didn't encounter any of the other archmages. They rarely ventured outside in winter, and as yet would have no reason to think anything had gone amiss with the Forging.

As he traipsed across frigid fields and into the nearest forest, Swift vowed to return to the castle one day. He'd slain one of the archmages responsible for the killing of apprentices, but there were still seven remaining. Seven wizards who had sacrificed younger and better mages to satisfy their own vanity.

It might take years, but they would pay for their crimes. Swift would see to that.

PRINCE OF BLOOD

GRISELDA HAD HEARD RUMOURS of war, but she found them hard to believe. The Convention—an elected group of wise and prominent citizens—had been set up to implement the King's laws, not to defy them. Was it really true that they had rebelled and taken up arms against their sovereign?

Her scepticism was soon swept away. The countryside was littered with symptoms of war: smouldering houses reduced to a few blackened sticks; detachments of armed men requisitioning barns to sleep in and food to devour; bodies piled high and burning in the fields. Violence seemed to have gripped the country like a fever.

Griselda tried to push these thoughts away as she approached Holdforth village. A local farmer called Skrint had called for a priest, and she'd come to answer the summons and offer what help she could. She was probably not exactly what he had in mind. She was a Priestess of the Shining Lady, a member of a small religious sect that many considered heretical. Despite the risks, they served their local communities as best they could, performing small services such as hypnotic healing and weather working. It was traditional white magic, but there was no escaping the fact that some people considered all magic to be dangerous and evil. She hoped Skrint wasn't one of those.

After asking a farmhand for directions, she found Skrint standing outside a barn, fixing a plough. He was a tall, stocky, man in late middle age. If the quality of his clothing was anything to go by, he was one of the more prosperous farmers in the area.

He leaned on his plough and looked Griselda up and down. 'I didn't think they allowed women into the priesthood,' he observed.

'I'm a *priestess*,' Griselda said, keeping her tone light and friendly. 'There are only a few of us, but we do the job as well as any man.' She didn't want to lie, but hoped to avoid admitting that she was not part of the official church.

Skrint looked sceptical, but he said, 'I suppose you'll have to do. No-one else has answered my summons. I hope you know how to deal with the dead.'

Griselda tried not to show how relieved she felt. 'I'm well versed in funeral rites.'

Skrint shook his head. 'Not funerals. I mean warding off the dead. Banishing fell spirits.'

Before she could ask what he meant, Skrint turned away and walked into the barn. Griselda assumed he wanted her to follow.

The barn was filled with a foul, cloying smell that almost made Griselda gag. In a corner, alongside a few mouldering pieces of farming equipment, an old man lay on a bed of straw. His clothes were dirty and ragged, his skin looked deathly pale, and his eyes were closed. Even at a distance Griselda could tell that he was dead, and had probably died some time ago. She knelt down beside him and touched his wrist to be sure. His skin was cold and there was no pulse.

'I'm glad to see you're not squeamish,' Skrint said.

'In wartime, can any of us afford to be?'

'Probably not. Although you might feel differently when you find out how he died.'

Griselda's eyes wandered to the man's torso. His shirt had been slashed open and there were deep gashes on his stomach and chest. She realised with a start that his wounds were still oozing blood. She watched some of it trickle down his side towards the sodden straw underneath him.

'When did he die?'

'A week ago.'

Griselda stood up and looked Skrint in the eye. She wasn't sure she'd got the measure of him yet. 'Are you joking?'

'I wouldn't joke about this. I can't say I knew this man well—he was a wandering vagrant as far as I know—but still. His name was Milton.'

The smell rising from Milton's body was almost overpowering. Griselda took a step back, not wanting to be sick or make a fool of herself in front of Skrint. It was important for the reputation of the Sisters of the Shining Lady that she be seen as calm, rational, and competent.

'Who is responsible for his injuries?'

Skrint jerked his head and stalked out of the barn. Griselda followed. They didn't speak again until they reached the nearby village of Holdforth, where Skrint led her into the local ale house. He exchanged a few quiet words with a serving girl, who sat down with them at a table. She had shoulder length blonde hair, a round face, and hazel eyes that were red around the edges. She sniffed as she sat down.

Griselda introduced herself and smiled in an effort to be friendly. 'I'm here to help,' she said.

The girl nodded tightly. 'I'm Eleanor.'

'Tell the priestess *exactly* what you saw,' Skrint said sternly.

'It happened three nights ago,' Eleanor said. 'I'd been working late and was hurrying home to be with Sam. We're not married yet, but we plan to be soon.' Her eyes were shining and she looked away for a moment to compose herself.

Skrint took up the story. 'There was a battle near the village about two weeks ago. Prince Leo came with an army to crush some rebels who were camped out near my land and who claimed to represent the Convention. Eleanor's quickest route home is across the battlefield. Unfortunately, neither side has bothered to collect their dead, so the area is littered with decaying bodies, abandoned where they fell.'

'Posing a serious risk of disease,' Griselda observed.

'Indeed.'

'Normally, I'd have gone around the battlefield,' Eleanor said, 'but I'd managed to buy some laudanum and I was desperate to get home to give it to Sam. He was hurt in the battle and is enduring a lot of pain.'

Eleanor looked stricken. Griselda felt bad for pressing her to continue, but if there was something dangerous prowling the battlefield, she needed to know about it. 'What did you see?'

The words came out in a rush. 'A tall man riding a warhorse, but no ordinary man. A spirit. A phantom on horseback.'

'Why do you believe he was a spirit, and not just an ordinary man?'

'Because I could see through him. It was very strange: the field was dark, but the man and his horse glowed like stained glass with the sun behind it. He was holding a sword that shone so bright I had to shade my eyes.'

'Did he hurt you?'

'For a moment I thought he was going to. I was rooted to the spot, frozen with fear. He rode to within a few paces and stared down at me. Then he said: "You are not my enemy", and rode off.'

Griselda studied Eleanor's face, trying to gauge both her truthfulness and her gullibility. Although the holy texts said that spirits sometimes lingered in the land of the living, they were exceedingly rare. False sightings were far more common.

'This is an upsetting time for you,' she said, patting Eleanor on the shoulder. 'And it was dark. Perhaps you simply saw a mortal man on horseback carrying a lantern, so that he appeared to glow?'

Eleanor shrugged off Griselda's hand. 'I know what I saw,' she said.

'Normally I'd share your scepticism,' Skrint said. 'But before he died, Milton staggered back to my farm babbling about a pale horseman with a gleaming sword. Then there are his wounds to consider. He died a week ago and yet they continue to bleed. How do you explain that?'

'Let's say this horseman was a spirit,' Griselda said, still full of doubts. 'What do you want me to do about it?'

Skrint's voice became suddenly harsh. 'You're a priestess, aren't you? Banish it; exorcise it. Or should I call for a male priest instead? Perhaps he would be better equipped for the job. I must say, I wasn't expecting a woman to answer my summons.'

Griselda ground her teeth and straightened in her seat. 'I'm more than capable, sir,' she said. 'I shall look into it, and *if* there is a spirit haunting the battlefield, I will deal with it. But I must be paid for my efforts.'

A mocking smile was playing at the corner of Skrint's mouth. He'd been trying to get a rise out of her, she realised. 'You'll be paid all right, don't worry about that. But only if you... *succeed*.'

Griselda felt a cold ripple of fear in her core. She had a nasty feeling that Skrint was really thinking: 'If you *survive*.'

DESPITE HER CONFIDENT WORDS, Griselda felt out of her depth. She hadn't been trained to hunt spirits, but she couldn't afford to back out now. Her sisters were counting on her to do a good job and enhance their reputation—or at least not do irreparable damage to it. The only way a group like theirs could survive was by doing good deeds and proving their value to the community.

In broad daylight, the battlefield was a grim sight. There were bodies everywhere and the air was thick with the reek of decomposition. Rats scurried gleefully among the corpses. There were gouges in the grass and scattered soil where artillery guns had ripped into the landscape. Griselda didn't know who had won the battle, but there had obviously been significant losses on either side. She looked away as a pair of squawking crows fought over the detached eyeball of a dead infantryman.

She noticed that some of the dead soldiers had been relieved of their weapons and valuables. The armies might be ignoring their dead, but the looters clearly weren't.

Although she remained sceptical, Griselda did not wholly discount the possibility that the spirit horseman was real, and that he might pose a threat to her. She did not plan to use herself as bait. Instead, she quickly set about making a scarecrow using some straw and rags that Skrint had provided. Then she hid in a nearby bush and remained there throughout the afternoon, hoping the spirit—if he existed—would come to investigate the scarecrow. But nothing happened. The field remained eerily still and quiet. Perhaps he would only appear after nightfall? Or perhaps the scarecrow was simply too crude to lure him out?

As dusk gathered, Griselda closed her eyes, prayed silently to the gods, then extended her hands and muttered words in an ancient language. The still air began to move. After a few minutes of concerted effort, she managed to rouse a wind strong enough to make the scarecrow sway. Then she stood up and shouted, throwing her voice so it would seem to come from the vicinity of the scarecrow. 'Show yourself, spirit! I challenge you to come out and face me!'

She did not really expect it to work. But it did.

The pale horseman materialised out of the air like a warm breath on cold glass. Even though Griselda could partially see through him, he looked like a strong, heavy-built man, sitting astride a black warhorse. There was a large X on his chest, and he carried a sword that shone like a beacon. He tugged on his horse's reins and trotted towards the scarecrow. Griselda crouched low, making sure she was hidden by the bush. As the horseman got closer, she saw that his bright sword was actually a sabre with a curved blade.

She inhaled sharply as she realised that he was not alone. Four more riders appeared and trotted behind their leader. They all wore uniforms marked with an X and were armed with long pikes.

Griselda had never seen a spirit before, never mind a whole company of them. Her mouth turned dry; her courage hung by a thread. *This was a terrible idea*, she thought. She decided to stay hidden in the bush and wait for the riders to depart. She could always return to confront them later with backup.

But the horseman had other ideas. Having inspected the scarecrow, he turned his blazing eyes towards the bush where Griselda was hiding. Her stomach turned over as she realised he could see her.

Blinded by panic, she squirmed out of the bush and sprinted towards Skrint's farm. She heard hoofbeats behind her and suddenly realised how foolish it was to try to outrun men on horseback. She quickly changed direction, jinking across the field in an effort to throw her pursuers off, but she tripped on one of the bodies and fell forward onto the cold ground. Soil and blood mixed in her mouth.

She pulled herself upright, panting hard, but the riders had already formed a circle around her and were pointing their pikes at her chest. Summoning what little courage she had left, she addressed the horseman with the glowing sabre, and said: 'I mean you no harm! I just wanted to speak to you and find out why you're here. *Please.*' The last word sounded like a sob.

The riders didn’t move or lift their pikes, but their leader tilted his head to one side, as if puzzling over what to do with her.

An idea bubbled to the surface of Griselda's mind.

You let my friend Eleanor go because you realised she wasn’t your true enemy,’ she said. ‘Well, I’m not your enemy either. I only came here to talk.’

‘I don’t want to talk,’ the leader said in a deep, rumbling voice. ‘But it’s true that you’re not the one I seek.’

He lowered his sabre. ‘I will spare your life if you bring my enemy back to me. Do that and you will have my gratitude. Fail to do so, and I will hunt you down and add your corpse to the multitudes already feeding the soil in this field.’

Griselda’s heart was drumming a frantic beat against her ribcage. ‘I’ll try,’ she said. ‘Who is your enemy? Where can I find him?’

But as soon as the rider had finished speaking, he began to disappear along with his fellow horsemen. For a moment it looked as if Griselda was surrounded by five puffs of swirling grey smoke. As the smoke dissipated, she saw something glittering on the ground where the lead rider had been. She hesitated, then went over to look at it.

It was a sabre—the one he had been holding. It no longer shone with spectral light, but it was still a stunning and beautiful weapon. The blade was fine and sharp and the hilt was inlaid with clusters of sparkling jewels. It was a weapon fit for a King.

GRISELDA HURRIED BACK TO the ale house with the sabre hidden under her clothes. She'd rented a room on the upper floor, and now she slipped upstairs quickly and quietly. She crept into bed and looked at the sabre under the bedclothes. It was easily the most magnificent object she'd ever seen. She couldn't even begin to imagine what it was worth in coin. More than she would ever see in her lifetime, probably. It was the kind of weapon that only a wealthy member of the nobility could have afforded. Which strongly suggested that the pale rider had been a nobleman, fighting on the King's behalf when he died. It seemed highly unlikely that any rebel could have afforded such a weapon. Even if they could, the Conventionists were known to prize modesty and restraint. Officers in their ranks wouldn't want to be seen with such an ostentatious weapon.

But why had the pale horseman left the sabre for her to find? What was she meant to do with it?

Valuable as it undoubtedly was, she could not sell it. It was simply too valuable and too unique. She knew no-one who could afford to buy it, and if she attempted to locate a buyer, she'd probably be robbed or arrested as a thief.

In their conversation, the pale rider had seemed to be obsessed with hunting down his enemy, whoever that might be. Had he given Griselda the sabre because it would help her to find his enemy?

She met Skrint downstairs at the bar the next morning. This time he didn't sit down, but stood staring at her with a stony expression on his face and his arms crossed over his chest. 'You failed to quell the spirit, I assume?' he asked.

'For now. But I did meet him and learn something of his intentions.'

Skrint raised an eyebrow. 'Which are?'

'He wants me to bring his enemy to him.'

'And who is that? Which poor devil has incurred the wrath of a homicidal spirit on horseback?'

Griselda bit her lip. 'Unfortunately, I don't know yet. But I mean to find out.'

Skrint sighed and rolled his eyes. 'Wonderful. So we have a vengeful spirit on our hands, and no way of sating his lust for violence. No wonder he's slain two people already. Did you find out *anything* useful?'

'There were five riders this time, all wearing armour marked with an X. Their leader was brandishing a sabre, which I assume is the same shining sword that Eleanor and Milton both saw.'

Griselda had decided in advance not to admit that the sabre was now in her possession. She didn't particularly trust Skrint, and didn't know what he might do with the information.

Skrint was frowning deeply. 'Your description doesn't make sense. The rebels marked their armour with an X in reference to the X that is drawn on a voting bill in the Convention—but only the King's men wielded sabres. The cavalry on the rebel side all carried spears. Still, it hardly matters. This horseman is clearly growing in strength and must be stopped before he kills again. I expect you want to back out, now that the situation has grown more perilous?'

There was a sneer in his voice, as if he'd always expected her to fail.

'Certainly not. I just need a few more days.'

'Very well. In the meantime, I will assemble some hardy men to face down this threat. Conduct your investigation—but be quick.'

With that, he tramped out of the ale house, his boots leaving a muddy trail on the floor.

Griselda chewed her breakfast of bread and marmalade thoughtfully. She didn't want to show the sabre to anyone, but how was she going to find the horseman's enemy without doing so? The more she thought about it, the more sure she was that the sword was a clue to the identity of the spirit's enemy.

She needed more information about the battle. At the very least, she ought to find out definitively what side the spirit horseman had been on.

Her eyes lighted on Eleanor, who was cleaning a glass behind the bar in a slow, desultory way. Her eyes glittered with unshed tears. Griselda approached the bar and asked if she was feeling alright.

Eleanor put down the glass and slumped forward on the bar, no longer able to stem the flow of tears. Griselda patted her awkwardly.

'I'm sorry,' Eleanor said, after blowing her nose. 'Sam is in so much pain, I can't bear it. His leg was shattered in the battle. It's become infected and needs to come off. I've been scouring the village for more laudanum, but it's all run out and I won't be able to get any more for at least a month.'

This was indeed a terrible dilemma. An amputation without pain relief was a dreadful thing. Sam could die from the pain alone.

'When is the operation going to happen?' Griselda asked.

'Tonight. The surgeon doesn't want to wait any longer.' Eleanor turned her tear-stained face towards Griselda, looking her straight in the eye. 'There's a rumour in the village that you know the ways of healing magic. Is that true?'

Griselda glanced around. Thankfully, there was no-one else in the ale house. 'If it were, I would not speak of it openly.'

'I don't blame you. Folk are suspicious of magic these days. There was a white witch in Holdforth when I was a small girl, but she was driven out. Still, if you know any healing arts—magical or otherwise—I beg you to help. I'll pay you every copper I can lay my hands on.'

Griselda was a skilled hypnotic healer. She had the power to blunt Sam's pain and make his dreadful ordeal more tolerable. Performing that kind of magic openly in a place like this was dangerous—for herself, and for her sisters—but how could she condemn a man to such an appalling fate, when she had the power to soothe him?

'Keep your coppers,' she said gently. 'You'll need them to buy more laudanum. In the meantime, I'll do everything I can to help Sam.'

THE SURGEON WAS A grim-faced man who treated his work like a military drill, but what he lacked in a bedside manner he made up for in efficiency. Griselda tried not to look too closely at his instruments, but the large hacksaw with serrated teeth was hard to ignore. She felt sick at the thought that it would soon be put to work on a frightened young man.

Worse, she knew that she too would feel its bite. Hypnotic healing involved connecting with the sick person on a deep, psychic level in order to soothe the parts of their mind that processed pain. As a result, she would likely feel some discomfort during the operation. It would only be a faint echo of the agony Sam would have to endure, but it was still a frightening prospect.

Sam lay in a single bed, with his eyes half open. He was young—no more than twenty, Griselda guessed—but he looked thin and pale. Eleanor had said he was apprenticed to the local blacksmith, but it was clear that his once strong muscles were beginning to waste away. The smell rising from his infected leg reminded Griselda of the rancid stink of Milton's decomposing body in the barn.

Sam's face was covered in a sheen of sweat and his eyes looked hollow and frightened, but as he became aware of Griselda and Eleanor entering the room, he made a visible effort to mask his fear.

'Thank you for coming, priestess,' he whispered.

Griselda moved her chair beside the bed and sat down. 'I'll try to block as much of your pain as I can, but I will not be able to get rid of it all. You must still brace yourself for agony. But I will be facing it with you, inside your mind. Try to open yourself to my presence.'

'I will,' Sam said through gritted teeth.

'You'll be tempted to try to shut everything out, including me. You must resist that temptation.'

Sam nodded grimly. There were unshed tears in his eyes.

'Will you hold my hand?' he asked.

'Of course.'

Griselda was sitting on Sam's right side. Eleanor sat down on his left. Two farmhands positioned themselves further down the bed on either side, ready to hold the patient down and stop him thrashing too much. Eleanor passed Sam a cup of brandy, her frightened expression mirroring his. He managed to knock back three full cups before the surgeon started work.

Griselda glimpsed a knife with a bright, clean blade in the surgeon's hand. She quickly turned her attention to Sam as the knife was brought into contact with the flesh of his leg. Sam shuddered and bit down hard on the scrap of leather in his mouth. Sweat rolled off his face and the farmhands soon had to grab him tightly to keep him still. Griselda gripped his hand tightly and tried to connect with his mind. It wasn't easy—his consciousness was like a frightened animal, skittering this way and that in a futile effort to evade the torment. His body convulsed and the farmhands grunted as they struggled to keep him restrained.

Griselda closed her eyes and spoke directly inside his mind.

I'm here, Sam. Listen to my voice and only mine. I will share this burden with you.

At first he tried to wrench away from her, but she repeated herself and the words eventually broke through his panic. His attention turned towards her.

Listen to my voice and only mine.

She felt him relax a fraction, enough for her to gently hold his consciousness and envelop it like a frightened sparrow held within cupped hands. With that, the hypnotic connection was made and the first step of Griselda's task was complete. Next, came the difficult part.

The pain assailed them both in waves. For Griselda, it was more like an acute memory of suffering than real pain, but it was still difficult to bear. She felt her body tense, her jaw tighten, her stomach churn. She focused on taking deep, slow breaths, knowing that Sam would remain calm if she did. She felt his consciousness slowly retreating from the reality of the situation. His pain was still bright and terrible, but his mind gradually disconnected from it.

That's it, Sam. We'll ride out the storm together.

Through her mind she felt his stuttering reply. *Thank you. Thank you.*

Although her eyes were still closed, she knew when the surgeon deployed his saw. It overrode the hypnotic block.

Sam screamed. Griselda let out a keening sob, before regaining control of herself.

It's nearly over. You're going to survive this and marry Eleanor.

The surgeon was mercifully quick with the saw and soon busied himself clamping shut the arteries and stemming the blood flow. Griselda opened her eyes a crack. She saw that he'd left a loose flap of skin, which he folded over the fleshy stump and sewed into place. When he was done, Griselda brought herself out of the hypnotic trance. A wave of nausea hit her immediately and she was almost sick. She crossed her arms over her stomach and rode it out.

'Will he make it?' Eleanor asked.

Sam looked utterly spent, but his heartbeat was still strong. The next few hours would be crucial.

'I don't know, but I think he has a good chance. He's young and determined. I'll stay with him all night.'

SAM FELL IN AND out of consciousness over the next few hours. The pain throbbed through his leg stump, and Griselda felt every pulse of it with him. She tried to remain conscious, but near dawn she fell asleep in her chair. Her dreams were vivid and strange. She saw thousands of armed men in neat rows, many with an X marked on their breastplate or sewn into their padded jackets. Cannons roared, filling the air with smoke and the smell of gunpowder. Men screamed. Some were blown to pieces, others charged into a storm of musket fire, their basket-hilted swords held above their bowed heads. A tall man on a black horse led a troupe of cavalry armed with pikes that flashed in the sunlight.

Griselda woke suddenly, breathing hard. To her surprise, she saw that Sam was awake and looking at her.

'I know who the rider is,' he said, his voice hoarse but purposeful.

'The pale horseman?'

Sam nodded, grimacing as he tried to prop himself upright.

'Don't strain yourself. 'You've been through a terrible ordeal.'

Griselda helped him up as Eleanor hurried into the room with a cup of water. When he'd drunk as much as he could manage, Sam said: 'Talking will help, I think. When Eleanor told me about this spirit rider, I immediately knew who it was, but I was in too much pain to explain. My mind is clearer now.'

Griselda smiled. Sam was still in terrible pain, she could feel it, but his spirit was strong and so was his desire to tell what he knew. There was no point in trying to dissuade him. In any case, she was eager to listen.

'You sustained your injuries during the battle between the rebels and the King's men, I understand. Which side were you on?'

'The side of the Convention. I joined up because the King has allowed rich and unscrupulous men to fence off our land and trample our natural rights as Burlishmen. I don't want to overthrow him, I just want him to listen to our just demands.'

'And what do you know of the spirit rider? I assume he was killed in the battle?'

Sam nodded. 'I believe he is—or was—a man called Hale. I met him while we were camping in the open air, waiting for Prince Leo's forces to arrive. He was a good man who brought his own horse to the battle. A natural leader. The kind of man you're glad is on your side.

'Over a cup of strong ale he told me he'd done well for himself before the war. He owned a fair slice of fertile farmland twenty miles from here, and made enough coin to feed, clothe, and educate his four children. His wife sadly died of consumption six years ago.

'He was elected to the Convention several times, and that seems to have been enough to mark him out for punishment by Prince Leo, who came through his village with a group of soldiers while Hale was away in the capital. Hale returned to find his house a smouldering ruin. The villagers told him that the prince locked his children inside, set the house on fire, then promised to torture and kill anyone who tried to rescue them.'

Eleanor tapped her chest just above her heart three times, a traditional gesture meant to invoke the mercy of the God of Light. Griselda didn't worship the God of Light, but she shared the sentiment.

'Did Hale hope to get revenge on the prince?'

'Most certainly. And he thought he would have an opportunity during the battle.'

Sam's voice was faltering, but he seemed determined to finish the story. Eleanor forced him to take a few more sips of water before he continued.

'I'm an artilleryman. We knew the royalist cavalry would try to outflank us and wipe out our guns at the first opportunity. Without artillery, we had little chance of winning the battle. Hale's horsemen were charged with protecting us. He believed Prince Leo would lead the attack on our flank personally with his dragoons. And he was right.

'The cavalry charge was terrifying. They surged towards us like demons out of the morning mist. The dragoons outnumbered Hale's men, but they were fighting uphill. I saw Hale knock the prince off his horse and duel him on foot. The prince is a skillful fighter, but Hale was stronger and driven by righteous rage. There was a look in his eyes that I cannot properly describe. Anger that was hot as the centre of a smithing stove but also terribly cold. He cut off the prince's hand with a stroke of his sword. He was about to sink the blade into the prince's neck when half a dozen dragoons on horseback came streaming back down the hill. They formed a circle around the prince and cut Hale to pieces.'

'You say Hale was armed with a sword? Was it a straight sword?'

Sam furrowed his brow. 'Yes.'

'And what about Prince Leo? What did he fight with?'

'All the dragoons were armed with sabres, but the prince had a special one, encrusted with jewels. I did wonder how practical it was, carrying a sword like that into battle. But the prince is nothing if not vain. He wanted to be seen and admired, I think.'

'Did he survive the battle? You said he lost his hand.'

Sam shrugged. 'I don't know. He was bleeding heavily, but his men would have done anything to keep him alive. My cannon exploded soon after Hale's death, so I didn't see much of what happened afterwards.'

'The prince is said to be recuperating in Eastwatch castle,' Eleanor said. 'A few miles from here.'

Griselda leaned back in her chair, letting out a long sigh. Her back groaned with pain from sitting up all night. Still, it was worth it, not only because Sam was alive, but because of what she'd learned. Hale's enemy was Prince Leo, younger son of the King, third in line to the throne. Killer of defenceless children. She realised she was shaking, not with fear or exhaustion, but with anger. She didn't doubt Leo's guilt. Even before the war, he'd had a reputation for brutality. It was one of the causes of the civil war. The prince believed he was above all laws and placed no value on the lives of commoners. But even by his low standards, burning the children in their beds was a crime of rare savagery.

She wondered what the wise women of her sect would counsel her to do in this situation. It was only an idle thought—she already knew she wasn't going to consult them. In the time it would take to solicit their advice, Hale would probably kill again, perhaps several times over. He might have been a good man in life, but what was left of him was dangerous and driven solely by a lust for blood and revenge. She had to act quickly.

'I found Prince Leo's sabre when I was scouring the battlefield,' Griselda said, making a quick decision to place her trust in Eleanor and Sam. 'As you rightly said, it's an ornate and valuable weapon. It should be returned to its rightful owner.'

Eleanor scowled. 'Didn't you hear what Sam said? The prince is a monster—a tyrant and a killer of children. He can do without his damned sabre!'

'You misunderstand me. The prince is indeed a monster, and some crimes demand justice, no matter how highborn the criminal. I mentioned his sabre because I want to use it to lure him back to the battlefield so that Hale's ghost can have his revenge.'

Eleanor gaped at her.

Sam grinned broadly. 'We'll help you,' he said. 'Damn the prince, and long live the Convention!'

His exhortation quickly turned into a cough that shook his body.

'You'll stay where you are and get some rest,' Eleanor said, before turning to Griselda. 'I'll fetch you pen and paper so you can write to the prince at Eastwatch castle. God of Light help us all.'

GRISELDA WROTE HER LETTER slowly and carefully. She wasn't especially used to writing, least of all to a prince, and she groped for a form of words that would compel him to come and collect his prize personally, rather than dispatching an underling. She struggled for a tone that was insistent and obsequious at the same time. She threw away several blotted drafts before finally finishing and giving the letter to Eleanor. She then said her goodbyes and left the house to return to her room at the ale house for some sorely needed rest. But there was a crowd waiting for her outside Sam and Eleanor's house. Skrint stood at the head of the group, scowling. Griselda shuddered. She guessed why they were here.

'You've had a busy night I see,' Skrint said, his arms crossed over his chest. 'I don't remember paying you to spend your time helping with matters of healing.'

'I don't remember you paying me anything at all.'

'I said I would when you rid us of the spectre on the battlefield. Have you done that?'

'I've made progress.'

Skrint sneered. 'Promises, promises. Did you find anything of interest when you visited the battlefield?'

There was a dangerous glint in Skrint's eye. Did he somehow know about the jewelled sabre? How?

'I will inform you when I have completed my task,' Griselda said coldly. 'For now, I need to take some rest before continuing my investigation.'

She tried to walk past the crowd, but they closed in on her, blocking her escape.

'Perhaps you'll understand better,' Skrint said, his voice low and dangerous, 'if I tell you that the land of the battlefield rightly belongs to me. It's adjacent to my farm and any plunder found there belongs to me also.'

'Unfortunately for you, that field is not full of booty,' Griselda said primly. 'It is full of dead young men, cut down in their prime. You should speak of them with more respect.'

'And you should speak with more honesty. You found a shiny sword there, did you not? When were you going to share that information with me?'

So he knew. 'When I return the sword to its rightful owner, Prince Leo.'

Skrint laughed, and a few of his pet thugs laughed with him. 'Hogwash! I think you're a thief masquerading as a priestess. I hired a boy,' Skrint jerked his thumb at a boy of perhaps ten who was standing next to him, 'to watch you do your work on the battlefield. Contacting the spirit. He watched you trade words with the evil spirit and then receive a jewelled sword for your troubles. That hardly sounds like you were trying to drive it off. What did you offer the creature in exchange for that bauble? The lives of all our children, perhaps? A free hand to terrorise our village?'

Before Griselda could answer the young boy pointed at her and shouted, 'She's a witch! I saw her wave her arms around and then a strange wind came up and blew everything about. It was so cold and horrible I thought I would die right there. She brought a scarecrow to life too!'

The crowd began mumbling ominously, closing in. Griselda turned on her heel and ran straight into a tall, muscular man who had been standing behind her. The impact left her winded. Suddenly the crowd were all around her, their hands grabbing pieces of her hair, her skirt, their spittle landing on her cheek. A heavy impact crunched against the back of her head and her vision went dark.

HOLDFORTH VILLAGE DIDN'T HAVE a jail, so Skrint chained Griselda up in an outbuilding on his farm with a dozen friendly brown pigs. Quite honestly, Griselda was grateful for the presence of the pigs, who nuzzled her with curiosity and kept her warm at night. After four days trying to squirm out of her chains, the skin around her wrists and ankles was raw and she was forced to give up on hopes of escape.

The boy that Skrint had used to spy on her brought her a heel of bread and a small cup of water once a day, but he had obviously been instructed not to speak to her. Her limbs ached from the lack of exercise and from the awkward position the chains forced her to sleep in.

After a week of incarceration, she awoke from a feverish dream to find a large group of men staring down at her. Skrint was there, looking uncertain, along with a handful of men from Holdforth. They were flanked by soldiers wearing leather coats and armed with short swords. At the head of the group of soldiers was a young man in black studded armour wearing a red sash tied around his waist and a wide-brimmed black hat. The hat had a red ostrich feather tucked into it and was worn at what might be considered a jaunty angle, but the young man's face was grim and serious. Griselda noticed that his right hand had been replaced with a brass replica, which peeked out from under his armour. She'd never seen anything like it before—it was beautifully designed, with four fingers and a thumb, and sculpted knuckles. She wondered if the brass digits could grasp and hold things, or if they were just for show.

Griselda was in no position to curtsy, but she inclined her head. 'Good morning, your majesty. Unfortunately I cannot stand to greet you properly.'

The prince frowned. 'Do you know me, wretched woman?'

Griselda shook her head. 'No, but I guess from your fine attire that you are Prince Leo. I heard you lost your hand in the recent battle.'

Prince Leo quickly moved his brass hand out of sight behind his back. 'This is the woman you plan to execute today?' He directed his question to the men from the village and spoke as if Griselda wasn't there.

Her heart began to beat frantically. Were the villagers really planning to execute her? For what? Trying to rid them of a dangerous spirit? But of course, if they believed she was a witch, they were bound by law to execute her. And what defence did she have? She had performed magic, in sight of a witness. She was an apostate who shunned the God of Light. She was guilty.

'She was seen consorting with an evil spirit,' Skrint said. 'But, your majesty, there's no need to waste your time with this trifling matter.' Skrint cringed as he spoke and his eyes were bulging. Judging by his expression, he had not known that the prince was coming to Holdforth, and was rather alarmed by Leo's arrival.

Dimly, her mind still heavy and feverish, Griselda realised that the prince had probably come here in response to her letter. That is, if Eleanor had still sent it after Griselda had been arrested. Whatever the case may be, her best chance of avoiding execution probably lay in appealing to Leo. The chains wouldn't allow her to stand up, but she got onto her knees and tried to adopt as dignified a pose as she could manage. Not an easy task, given how filthy and famished she was.

'Your majesty, I swear I am not a witch. I came here to help the people of Holdforth drive away the fell spirit Skrint spoke of. Indeed, I was employed by Mr Skrint for that very task. I'm not sure why he has turned against me so violently.'

'Because you were seen performing magic and making a deal with the spirit,' Skrint growled.

Skrint looked like he was about to say more, but Prince Leo silenced him with a stern look. He then looked at Griselda and said, 'Are you the woman who wrote to me at Eastwatch?'

Griselda felt a wave of relief. Eleanor had sent the letter after all. That gave her a glimmer of hope.

‘I am. I found a precious sabre, studded with gems, on the battlefield, which I believe belongs to you. I felt you should have it back.’

‘Where is the sabre now?’

‘Skrint stole it!’ Eleanor shouted, elbowing her way to the front of the group. She then seemed to realise what kind of company she was in and attempted to curtsy for the prince, although there wasn’t really enough room to do so. ‘I swear it, my lord. Griselda wanted to return the sword to you, but Skrint stole it and has been making plans to sell it.’

Leo turned on Skrint, his eyes dark and full of menace. ‘I want the truth now,’ he said. ‘Do you have my sabre?’

Skrint cringed so much it looked for a moment as if he was about to get down on hands and knees. ‘I only kept it for safekeeping, your majesty. I can fetch it for you now. It’s in perfect condition!’

Leo narrowed his eyes. ‘And yet I received no letter from you, only from this wretch.’

One of the prince’s bodyguards laid a gloved hand on Skint’s shoulder, holding him in place while the prince studied him.

‘Now that you see the truth, your majesty, I hope you will grant me your pardon,’ Griselda said, trying to keep her voice calm and respectful.

Leo scowled and spat on the barn floor. ‘I don’t like thieves,’ he said. ‘And I don’t like witches either.’ He nodded towards his men. ‘Take them both into the village square and execute them. That will put an end to this nonsense.’

‘No—please!’ Griselda cried. ‘I haven’t told you the whole story yet.’

Her mind was racing. What was she going to say? What would be compelling enough to persuade him not to execute her?

‘Haven’t told me what?’

‘The spirit said there were other things lost on the battlefield that ought to be recovered.’

‘What other things?’

‘Important documents. Notes from rebel commanders detailing troop movements and locations for future attacks. I believe the spirit is one of your fallen comrades who wishes for you to have these papers, or else he fears you might lose the war. If you take me back to the battlefield, I will call on your comrade so you can recover these important items.’

Leo tipped his head back and laughed. 'What rubbish women will speak to save their own skin! I don't believe in this spirit, and I doubt that my enemies can read and write, nevermind formulate written battle plans. But the battlefield is as good a place as any to hang a thief and a witch, so we will go there and see what your tale amounts to.'

'A most excellent plan,' Skrint simpered, bowing his head and staring at the prince's feet. 'And once you have satisfied yourself that this witch is lying to you—'

'Once I have satisfied myself about that, I will hang you both. Men, bring these two with us, and don't forget to bring a rope and scaffold from the village.'

GRISELDA STARED AT THE scarecrow. It looked shabby and dishevelled, but it was still intact. This was where she'd encountered Hale's ghost before, but she'd had to resort to weather magic to attract his attention. Surrounded by the prince's men, and other men from the village, she couldn't risk using magic again. It would only make them even more certain she was a witch.

She desperately willed Hale to show himself again. *I've done as you asked,* she thought desperately. *I've brought your enemy back to you. Where are you?*

'I've had enough of this,' Leo said. 'She's obviously lying to try to save her own skin. There never was a spirit. Put up the scaffold and let's get this over with.'

Before she could even think about running, two soldiers grabbed her roughly and twisted her arms behind her back, while the villagers erected a crude scaffold. As they were doing so, a new group arrived on the field. Eleanor was among them, as was Skrint, who was flanked by two soldiers. His face was pale and he was shivering in the wind. The bejewelled sabre was in his hands.

'Here is your sword, your majesty,' he said in a quavering voice. 'I've kept it safe for you.'

'You kept it safe for yourself,' snapped the prince. 'Take him to stand with the witch and bring me the sabre.'

His soldiers obeyed at once. The prince soon had the sabre in hand and Griselda and Skrint were led onto the rickety scaffold. It was not very high, which did not make it less frightening. Their necks were unlikely to break with such a short drop, which meant they were being condemned to a slow death by strangulation.

Lengths of rope were tied to the top of the scaffold and then looped around their necks. Skrint started babbling, begging for mercy. Griselda felt sick.

'Get on with it,' Leo shouted. 'I don't want to stand about in this filthy graveyard all day.'

'She's done nothing wrong!' Eleanor shouted, looking both distraught and furious. 'You can't execute loyal citizens without a trial! Even Skrint deserves a fair hearing, although he's a toad and a thief.'

A few of the other villagers nodded, although most looked too scared to object.

'Shut that wretch up now, or bring her up here to join the witch,' Leo barked. 'I daresay there's a whole coven of them in this benighted place.'

A couple of soldiers moved to lay hands on Eleanor, but she wasn't finished yet. 'You're a monster!' she shouted. 'A man of blood! A child killer! Those who are drowning in blood don't deserve to call themselves princes.'

The soldiers finally reached Eleanor. One of them stuffed a piece of cloth in her mouth and the other punched her in the stomach. She doubled over, coughing through the improvised gag. To Griselda's immense relief, the prince didn't demand that she be brought to the scaffold too. He simply waved for his men to get on with the hangings they had already planned.

A soldier stepped onto the narrow plank and pushed Skrint off. He swung around, pawing uselessly at the noose around his neck, making dry, gasping sounds in his throat. As his body turned, Griselda saw that his face was turning purple and there were burst blood vessels in his eyelids.

In their hurry to get on with the execution, the soldiers had forgotten to bind their hands. She realised that gave her one last, faint thread of hope. She raised her hands and moved them around, muttering the secret words she had been taught that called upon the old, abandoned gods to intervene in the mortal world. She was shivering in the cold and stumbled on some of the words, but the spell worked. A fierce wind leapt up, out of nowhere. The small crowd of villagers and soldiers gasped as the wind whipped their clothes and the scarecrow danced like a festival puppet.

The prince was the first to come to his senses. 'What in the King's name are you waiting for?' he barked. 'Kill the witch!'

Griselda felt a hand on the small of her back. She was shoved off the scaffold and the breath was pushed out of her mouth in a rush. The rope bit painfully into her neck and her head snapped forward. Her vision swam and she almost passed out. She tried to draw breath but could only make a rasping sound. Panic flooded her body. She kicked and thrashed uselessly in the air. She tried to breathe through her nose, but it did her no good as her airway was crushed.

The crowd of villagers and soldiers stared at her, some grinning, most looking forlorn and shaking their heads. None moved to help her or Skrint. Eleanor tried to shout something through her gag, but one of the soldiers cuffed her on the head and she fell silent. The prince looked bored. Far behind him, the fierce wind seemed to have turned into a soupy, thick fog that grew more dense with each passing moment.

It wasn't fog, Griselda realised. It was the pale horseman and his men.

Hale.

He gripped the reins of his black horse and charged at the prince.

The crowd suddenly realised what was happening. They parted and several people screamed. Some of the soldiers drew their swords but others hesitated, clearly wondering what good their weapons would be against a group of phantoms. Prince Leo wheeled around, called his men to him, and backed away from Hale, holding his jewelled sabre aloft, as if to ward off the evil approaching him.

Hale sped past the prince, who stumbled but appeared to be uninjured. Hale continued on and stopped next to the scaffold. Griselda now saw that he had taken the jewelled sabre from Leo. It shone like a star in his hand as he cut Griselda down.

She fell to the ground hard and spent a good while wheezing on the ground, consumed by pain, but giddy with relief. Eleanor rushed up and helped her to her feet.

As Griselda recovered her wits, she saw that Hale had climbed off his horse and was standing over her.

'Thank you,' he said. His booming voice seemed to echo inside her mind.

She nodded, and Hale got back on his horse. His comrades gathered around him, a tight-knit cavalry brigade, well-drilled and disciplined even in death.

Skrint was still hanging from the scaffold, his face dark purple. Eleanor had a paring knife and, with difficulty, they cut him down.

By the time that was done, the prince and his soldiers had taken a defensive position, although they looked terrified.

Hale and his men charged.

Griselda scrambled back onto the scaffold and shouted at the top of her lungs. 'This quarrel is between the phantoms and Leo, child-killer. There's no need for anyone else to die for this bloody prince.'

It worked. One by one, the soldiers peeled away from their commander, running back towards the village, until Leo was left alone, his mouth open, his eyes round with terror.

Hale separated Leo's head from his neck with a single, precise stroke of the sabre. A spray of blood erupted from the wound and painted a red arc on the grass. Leo's body fell limp to the ground.

Hale turned around and returned to the scaffold, dropping the sabre at Griselda's feet. 'I have no more need for this,' he said, before galloping away across the field with his comrades. As they rode, they shed pieces of themselves until all that could be seen was a grey haze hanging between the mud and the sky.

Griselda's head was spinning.

What was she going to do with this sabre?

What was she going to do with herself? Stay in Holdforth for a while or flee immediately?

Skrint was still wheezing, but he was beginning to recover himself and stood up. She wondered if his brush with death had taught him any wisdom. Probably not. More likely, he would be more determined than ever to punish Griselda for having the temerity to save his life.

She returned briefly to Eleanor's house, thanking her for her help, stocking up on provisions, and saying goodbye to her and Sam. It was high time to return to her fellow priestesses, she decided. Let *them* decide what to do with the jewelled sabre.

They would want to stay out of the conflict that was engulfing the country, but Griselda now felt sure they would be sucked into the civil war one way or another. If the events at Holdforth were anything to go by, they could at least count on the old gods being on their side.

A RARE DELICACY

Tybil was growing impatient. He'd been sitting in a shadowy corner of the tavern nursing the same flagon of ale for over an hour. Where the hell was Rickard?

The shadows lengthened, the tavern grew busier, until at long last Rickard bounced into the tavern with an irritating grin on his face. He greeted Tybil expansively with a mock bow.

'Shut your mouth and sit down,' Tybil growled. 'You're late.'

'Can't be helped,' Rickard said cheerfully. 'Have you seen the King's Parade yet? It really is extraordinary. Enough to make a man feel intensely patriotic! The whirling spice dancers are especially—'

'Enough babbling!' Tybil hissed. 'Time is short and there are spies everywhere. You said you have something that will suit our purpose?'

Rickard's grin grew wider. 'I've outdone myself this time, Tibs, I really have!'

A knot of men with steely eyes and steelier broadswords were standing near the bar. One of them eyed Tybil and Rickard with curiosity.

'Keep your voice down, for pity's sake.'

Rickard continued at the same volume, seemingly unaware of, or unconcerned by, the armed men at the bar. 'Trust me, Tibs, you'll want to sing with joy when you see it.'

Despite his nervousness and frustration with his friend, Tybil felt a flush of excitement. This could, after all, be the big break he'd been searching for. A surefire way to curry favour with the new King. His ticket into the privy council. No more scrimping and saving. No more long nights freezing his balls off patrolling the walls of the city. Power and wealth might finally be within his grasp.

'What is it?' he whispered. 'A contraption of war? An elixir of eternal life? The secret of alchemy?'

Still grinning, Rickard overturned his saddle bag and something heavy and wet flopped onto the table. A hunk of bloody meat.

'A steak? That's it?'

Rickard leaned forward. 'Ah, but this is no ordinary steak. It was carved from the hindquarters of a dragon!'

Tybil eyed the meat suspiciously. Blood was oozing out of it, sinking into the grooves of the wooden table. It didn't look any different from any other steak he had seen, except perhaps that there seemed to be a glossy sheen to the red blood coming out of it, like oil glistening on the surface of water.

'Rickard, we need a present for the King that will rival gifts from his richest, cleverest, and most sycophantic courtiers. Does it at least taste good?'

Rickard threw up his hands. 'The taste is irrelevant! You're missing the point entirely, my friend. If the King eats this while it is fresh and bloody, he will gain the strength of a thousand men! The guile of a hundred courtiers! Not to mention'—Rickard winked lasciviously—'a potency that his lady queen will find most gratifying.'

Tybil opened his mouth to argue, then closed it again. Perhaps Rickard was onto something, after all. *A dragon steak!*

It certainly sounded like a kingly gift, but would it really convey the powers he described?

Tybil stared down at the meat, following the faint tracery of veins with his eyes and watching as the moat of blood around the outside thickened and turned black. The blood looked even more like dark oil glistening on the tabletop.

'You've gone mad, Rickard,' he said. 'The King will think we are trying to poison him and have us instantly arrested. Get out of here—I will dispose of this revolting morsel and save us both from the executioner's block.'

The two men argued fiercely for several minutes, but Rickard eventually relented and stormed out of the tavern, leaving the steak behind.

Tybil's heart drummed against his ribcage.

The power of a thousand men!

The potency of a man half his age!

When he was sure he wasn't being overlooked by anyone else in the tavern, he bit down hard on the steak. The meat was chewy and had a nasty, smoky aftertaste, but it was nothing to a man who had eaten fried rat while on night watch. Tybil persevered with his meal, washing the whole thing down with the dregs of his ale.

It wasn't long before his stomach growled ominously. Sweat rolled off his chin. He gripped the table and gritted his teeth.

As he stood up, a huge, rumbling belch forced its way up his throat. The burp suddenly ignited as it left his mouth, producing an immense tongue of flame that twisted through the air and lashed the tavern's wooden beams, setting them ablaze. The fire spread quickly, leaping between gaps in the timber as if animated by a desire to consume the building as quickly as possible. Tybil was dimly aware of the other patrons screaming and running for the exit, but there was nothing he could do to prevent the unfolding disaster. Fire continued pouring out of him, unbidden.

A while later, when the fire breath had finally abated, Tybil emerged from the smouldering wreckage of the tavern. His clothes were reduced to a few charred flaps of cloth, but he was unhurt. Glossy green scales had erupted on his face and neck. His sweaty, smoke-blackened face had an oily sheen to it.

Shivering and bewildered, Tybil left the city behind and began climbing the nearest mountain where, according to legend, a dragon had once made its nest.

THE LADY IN THE LOCKET

THE CUSTOMS HOUSE WAS just as Sofia remembered it. The only thing that distinguished it from a common roadside inn was the red-and-white Burlish flag that hung from a flagpole above the entrance. The local customs man—Hobbs—showed her into a sitting room containing two wingback armchairs and a bearskin rug stretched in front of a roaring fire. She heard him turn the key in the lock on his way out. There were no other doors through which she might leave the sitting room and there were brass bars across the windows.

Sofia draped her travelling cloak over the arm of her chair. She'd been cold on the ship, and even colder as she'd tramped along the beach and up the muddy path to the customs house, but now she was warm. Too warm. She wiped her face with a handkerchief that was grimy from the journey.

Hobbs returned a few minutes later with a salt beef sandwich on a copper plate and a glass of Burlish red wine that tasted like sour jam and made Sofia's head swim when she sipped it. He sat down and watched while she ate. Hobbs was a tall, thickset man with a handlebar moustache and small, dark eyes. His coat and waistcoat were the same colour as the wine. Chunky gold rings adorned his swollen fingers.

Sofia hurried through her meal as quickly as she could without making a mess. When she'd finished eating, Hobbs asked what had brought her to his customs house on such a cold night.

'I'm trying to escape Onteel,' she said. 'I crossed the Haven Strait on a merchant ship and hope to find sanctuary here, under the Burlish flag.'

If Hobbs was surprised by her candour, he didn't show it. 'What are you fleeing from?' he asked.

'A marriage.'

'You do not want to be married?'

'I do not. But my father feels otherwise.'

'And who is your father?'

Sofia looked down at her roadworn boots. 'A leather merchant in Greyhaven. A man of no importance.'

The fire crackled. Sofia felt Hobbs watching her from under his bushy eyebrows. After several breaths of silence he took hold of her chin and lifted her gaze to meet his. His hands were warm and rough but the rings on his fingers were cool and hard and pressed painfully into her jaw. She saw now that his eyes were not dark at all, but flinty and grey.

'Your father is not a leather merchant,' he said. 'Tell me the truth.'

Sofia swallowed hard and fingered the gold locket around her neck. 'My father is... the Duke of Onteel.'

Hobbs' eyes glittered with triumph. He smiled and dropped his hand from Sofia's chin to her knee. 'I suspected as much. You'll be safe here, I promise. Have no fear.'

Sofia tried not to flinch from his touch. 'You won't turn me in? My father has offered a large reward for my return. I'm sure he is furious with me.'

Hobbs moistened his lips with the tip of his tongue. 'Your secret is safe with me, my dear,' he murmured.

How long will it take him to dash off a note and send it to Greyhaven? Sofia wondered. *How long before the Duke's men are hammering at the door? Only a fool would trust him...*

‘I wish I had some coin to repay your hospitality,’ she said, ‘but unfortunately I was robbed at the docks. Let me offer you this as payment instead.’

Sofia unclasped her gold locket and handed it to Hobbs. It was a fine piece of jewellery, although most of the floral design on the lid had worn away from too much handling.

‘There is no need, really,’ he said, turning the locket over and feeling its weight in his hand. As he did so it fell open, revealing the portrait inside. Hobbs tried to appear composed, but Sofia saw him flinch when he laid eyes on the lady in the locket.

‘That’s my aunt,’ she said, with a touch of pride. ‘She was the terror of our family for years. She once worked for my father, but then she lost her mind and started handing out curses as if they were dragonfly cakes.’

‘She looks entirely mad,’ Hobbs said, ‘with her wild hair and staring eyes. I find it hard to believe she’s a relative of yours.’

‘I have her eyes, I think. She fled Onteel years ago after stealing the Duke’s best silver and a portion of his fortune. She was never seen again.’

Hobbs stared at the portrait for a long time. The wheels were turning in his mind. He was probably sifting through his memories, but if so, he said nothing of it to Sofia and asked no further questions. He closed the locket and put it down on the arm of his chair.

A housekeeper entered the sitting room soon after, bringing whiteberry tarts and a bottle of brandy on a silver tray. Hobbs poured them each a glass, and together they toasted her perilous journey from Grayhaven to the Burlish border. Sofia smiled and fluttered her eyelashes and continued drinking with Hobbs until his cheeks turned pink and he drew his armchair alongside hers.

'This has been a lovely evening, don't you think?'

'I do.'

Hobbs drained his third glass of brandy and smacked his lips. 'Can I tell you a secret?' he said. 'I met your aunt once. Years ago. She was mad as a hen. Mad as a barrel of peas.'

'I thought you might have,' Sofia said eagerly. 'She fled this way, I understand, seeking aid from the Burlish after she robbed my father. What happened? I hope you caught her!'

'I did,' Hobbs said with relish. 'I confiscated her stolen goods: a bag full of silverware and a purse heavy with gold. The biggest haul of my career!'

'That can't have been easy. My father told me she was a witch. A real spellsinger.'

Hobbs nodded vigorously. 'She was a witch, and a fearsome one at that. It took twenty men from the village to subdue her.'

Sofia prodded him playfully. 'Shouldn't you have granted her asylum? Isn't that your duty as a Burlish official? It can't have been easy for her to cross the border alone.'

'Certainly not. That's not my job. I collect taxes for Burland, but I also have an arrangement with your father to intercept and return outlaws fleeing his dukedom. I was well within my rights to arrest her.'

Hobbs suddenly realised what he'd said and looked away. He'd tipped his hand without meaning to. It would be obvious now to even the dullest mind that he intended to return Sofia to the Duke and collect the reward. And Sofia's mind was far from dull, even after several glasses of liquor.

The time had come to act.

The gold locket was still lying on the arm of Hobbs' chair. Sofia reached over and touched it. The cool, smooth gold turned suddenly hot; the locket felt like a stone plucked from the embers of a fire. A ripple of energy climbed up Sofia's arm and settled in her core. Her body began to morph and rearrange itself into a new shape. Her soft, plump skin sagged and her hair grew out and turned grey. She let out a long, satisfied breath as the transformation spread from the tip of her nose to the joints in her fingers and toes. It was a relief to finally shed the illusion of youth. It had taken a lot of effort to sustain.

Hobbs' mouth fell open. 'You..?'

Sofia nodded. Hobbs lurched to his feet, but before he could take any action a sound like the cracking of thunder filled the small sitting room. The furniture vibrated and the room fell dark, as if someone had draped a black cloth over it. Sofia heard Hobbs fall back into his chair and let out a long, wheezy breath. She reached for the locket again, groping for it in the dark. It was now warm rather than hot, and pulsed in her hand like a beating heart.

The room returned to its normal illumination. Hobbs was slumped in his chair, his body limp, his head lolling back, his eyes blank and lifeless.

Sofia quickly gathered up her things and left the customs house. Once she was several miles away and confident she wasn't being followed, she stepped off the main road and into a wood where she sat with her back against a tree. She took a match out of a box in her travelling bag and struck it. The flame fizzed and then burnt steadily. She opened the locket and looked inside. Hobbs stared back at her in portrait form, his mouth slightly open, his grey eyes wide with fear.

Sofia smiled and snapped the locket shut.

DRAGON SIGHT

Ciana found a delivery of beeswax waiting for her on the street outside the shop when she rose in the morning. Dawn was streaking the sky with orange and blue, backlighting the low stone buildings that crowded the city's industrial quarter. There had been fresh snowfall in the night, leaving the streets muffled and white. Ciana shivered in the biting cold as she dragged the heavy wooden box into the backroom and levered it open with a crowbar, filling the shop with a rich, earthy, sweet scent. She lit a fire underneath the cauldron hanging in the hearth and lifted one of the beeswax blocks into it. While waiting for the wax to melt she tidied the shop, flung open the window shutters, washed her face, and ate a breakfast of stale bread and cheese. Her father had left the shop early, as he often did these days, beginning his long climb to the upper levels of the city before dawn.

Not for the first time, Ciana wondered why they lived in poverty when her father worked as an advisor to the Duke of Onteel, the wealthiest man in Greyhaven.

'Wealth attracts unwanted attention,' her father often said. 'The aristocracy rarely deign to visit the lower levels of the city, and when they do they avert their eyes from the poor. Which suits us well.'

Ciana didn't long for the life of a pampered aristocrat, but was it necessary that they sleep in splinter-ridden palettes when their employer wore silk pyjamas and commanded an army of servants? Despite the success of their business—and the Duke's political ascendency—they seemed poorer than ever.

The beeswax bubbled, filling the room with a sweet, smoky aroma. Ciana took a tray filled with fresh wicks weighted on one end and dipped them in the cauldron, one after the other, layering up the wax, before hanging the candles from a ceiling beam to cool. Through the windows she glimpsed tradesmen traipsing past on the street outside, wading through snow and wishing one another good morning. A few customers came in to buy boxes of candles and warm themselves in front of the hearth.

Ciana and her father traded in two commodities: candles, and information. What no-one else knew was that the two sides of their business were intimately connected.

Most of the candles were sold to wealthy customers; the poor had to make do with cheap tallow alternatives that emitted thick, black smoke and stank of animal fat. Once made, each candle was placed inside a device which stamped a unique number onto its base. Before removing the candle, Ciana would copy the number into a ledger along with the name of the intended customer. There was also a place in the ledger for noting the room in which the candle had been placed, but this information would be added later.

As the first of the new candles cooled to room temperature, Ciana took one and placed it in the numbering device. As she did so, the candle wick burst into flame, burning with an intensity that suggested it was fuelled by more than beeswax vapour.

A deep voice rumbled, 'Your father is lying to you, Ciana.'

The candle flared; the flame rose high above the wick. Within its yellow centre, Ciana glimpsed the dark outline of an eye. To most it would seem like a trick of the light, a passing shadow, but she had seen the eye before and knew what it represented.

'My father keeps information from me, Thorn, for my own safety. That isn't the same as lying.'

'A meaningless distinction. Your father doesn't trust you with his secrets.'

'I've helped with his information work. I know more about the workings of the Duke's inner circle than almost anyone in the city.'

That was only partially true; Ciana's father rarely confided in her, and seemed less willing to do so with each passing month.

The dark eye narrowed. 'Those are other people's secrets. Your father has his own, of which you know nothing, though they may yet change the course of your life. Or bring it to a painful end.'

Ciana couldn't help herself. She took the bait. 'What secrets?'

The candle flared brighter.

'I'm willing to show you.'

Ciana hesitated. She knew what Thorn meant. He could show her what he saw through the candle flames. It was something she had discovered a year ago, soon after Thorn began speaking to her directly. She did not know if her father could do as she could—commune directly with Thorn and share his sight—but she suspected not. She'd intended to tell her father about this, but had somehow never gotten around to it.

Her father had his secrets.

Ciana had a few of her own.

'Well? Has my generous offer dazzled your young mind?'

'No,' Ciana said sharply. 'No deal. I'm not interested in playing your stupid games.'

Before he could reply, she pinched out the candle flame with her index finger and thumb, sending Thorn back into oblivion.

Arturo returned late that evening. There were dark circles under his eyes. Despite the lateness of the hour, he set about his usual ritual, brushing the snow off his clothes and shaving with a pocket razor in front of a mirror that hung by the door. Ciana watched him from the storage room, where she'd been tidying away the newly crafted candles into boxes ready to sell. Her father looked thin and pale, his skin like a bedsheet stretched too tight over the bones of his face. Lately, he'd been leaving the shop before dawn and returning home long after sunset. She rarely saw him eat. There was a crack in the mirror he was shaving with, and Ciana remembered that he used to have a larger one with a gilt frame, a gift from the Duke. He must have sold it without telling her. Did he think she wouldn't notice these things?

Ciana stepped out of the storage room, carrying a lit candle in an iron holder. There was no sign of the dark eye within the flame, but Ciana wondered if Thorn was there nonetheless, watching, listening, calculating.

'How is the Duke?' she asked.

'As happy and boisterous as ever,' Arturo said, inspecting the stubble on his chin.

Boisterous? Did he mean the Duke had been violent? It seemed an odd choice of word, one that might be freighted with hidden meaning.

Ciana balled her fists in frustration. She was always forced to play this game with her father—interpreting his cryptic remarks, reading meaning into his silences. He rarely gave direct answers to her questions, certainly not if the question touched on the Duke, or her father's information gathering work. On the rare occasions he did confide in her, she observed him first calculating the value and risk of bringing her into his confidence before uttering a word.

She was his daughter, his only family. Why didn't he trust her?

'I made stew for dinner. Would you like some?'

'That's good of you, but I'm not hungry. I shall look forward to eating it cold in the morning.' His voice was flat, emotionless.

'You'll waste away if you don't eat.'

Arturo looked at her wearily. 'I eat well enough at the Duke's expense.'

'I doubt that. When are you planning to tell me about our money problems? You've sold most of our possessions over the last few months, yet you seem to think I won't notice. Have you fallen out of favour with the Duke? Is Thorn refusing to follow your instructions?'

Arturo turned to face her properly now, pocketing the shaving knife. There was a warning in his eyes. They rarely talked openly about Thorn and the candles, even when alone together in the shop.

'We always have problems of one sort or another, which I am used to dealing with. Selling a few possessions does not mean we are destitute. Our businesses continue to prosper—both of them—and will continue to do so as long as we each attend to our respective duties.'

His meaning was clear: *you concern yourself with candle making and let me worry about gathering information for the Duke.*

Ciana knew she was intelligent and resourceful. She had a good grasp of Greyhaven politics and a capacity for ruthlessness—perhaps more so than her father, who sometimes hesitated when he should act decisively. She was certain she'd be good at gathering and deploying intelligence, yet he didn't allow her to even try. It was infuriating.

Arturo tidied himself up after shaving and wished Ciana goodnight, clearly keen to bring their conversation to a swift end. Ciana went to bed a short while later knowing she'd have a hard time getting to sleep.

Her mother would never have put up with this, Ciana thought while staring at her bedroom ceiling. She'd died nine years ago, when Ciana was twelve years old. Where Arturo was kind, quiet, and a deep thinker, Ciana's mother had been intense, passionate, decisive. She was the one responsible for the candle magic that now sustained their livelihood and the Duke's power.

Ciana had not been present when her mother had captured Thorn's spirit, but she knew the spell had gone wrong somehow, rebounding on the one who cast it. Even at twelve years old, she'd had an inkling her mother and father were hatching a plan to lift the family out of poverty and give them a secret weapon in a city where the rich took whatever they pleased and the poor had to scramble to survive. As it turned out, the cost of capturing Thorn's spirit and placing it within the candles had been Ciana's mother's life. She'd died in the darkness of a damp cave on the side of a mountain, surrounded by a circle of guttering candles.

A sudden noise brought Ciana back to full waking. A floorboard creaking outside her bedroom.

A surge of fear swept through her. Her first thought was that the person must be a burglar who had come to raid the shop, or worse, an assassin come to kill her father. She grabbed the dagger she always kept beside her bed, rose silently, crept to her bedroom door and pressed her eye to the keyhole. It was hard to see much in the darkness, but she detected no movement in the shadows. Someone might be hiding, though.

Bracing herself for a fight, Ciana thrust open her bedroom door and stepped out, ready to strike with the dagger. But the shop was empty, and nothing looked amiss. The candles were neatly stacked where she'd left them. She scanned every corner, but everything looked as it should do.

Her father had his own room, which was really a small storage cupboard that he'd squeezed a sleeping palette into.

'Father?'

There was no reply—no sound at all. Ciana's heartbeat thundered in her ears. She pushed the door open and peered inside. There was the palette with a thin blanket neatly draped on top. Her father wasn't there, nor was there any sign of a struggle. On the contrary, it looked as though he'd tidied up after himself before leaving his bedroom.

The implications of this settled over Ciana. Why was her father sneaking out in the middle of the night? What business took him outside in the dead of night, when he'd already spent all the daylight hours working at the Duke's court?

Back in the public area of the shop, a candle had ignited above the hearth.

'Your father's deception continues,' Thorn said, 'but it will come to an end sooner or later. What will you do when he is dead and you are destitute?'

Ciana didn't reply to Thorn's goading, but went into the storage room and brought some extra wood and kindling to the hearth, which she lit it with the candle. Bringing a chair over to the fire, she sat down and stared into the flames. The dark eye was there in front of her, larger than ever, almost as big as the fireplace itself. At this size, she could make out more detail. The eye was surrounded by scales and the pupil was a vertical black slit.

'Show me,' she said, folding her hands in her lap. 'Show me what my father is hiding from me.'

The eye winked out of existence and Ciana's vision blurred. She felt dizzy and weak; her stomach churned and her body felt weightless and clammy. She doubled over, hugging herself and hoping she wouldn't be sick.

The shop dissolved into darkness around her.

As the feeling of weightlessness faded, Ciana found herself standing in a large cave. The eye from the fireplace was still in front of her, but now it was attached to a green and silver scaled dragon who was curled up on a carpet of gold coins.

The smell of smoke and sulphur hung in the air. Hundreds of candles lined the edges of the cave, some lit, some dark. They stood several layers deep, some standing close to the ground in puddles of wax, others almost touching the cave's low ceiling.

Ciana steadied herself, determined not to show any weakness. 'What do you want to show me?'

'A great deal.'

Thorn remained curled up like a cat in a basket, but with his tail he pointed to a specific candle in a tall candlestick. Ciana fetched the candlestick and brought it to the middle of the cave. Staring into the candle flame, she saw the cave dissolve in her peripheral vision, just as her father's shop had dissolved, the bright rows of candles winking out of existence. The feeling of dizzy weightlessness returned, but Ciana was prepared for it and didn't feel quite so overwhelmed.

In place of the cave, she saw a library full of leather bound books in tall, oak bookcases. There were brass ladders on runners attached to the bookcases, and a couple of damask sofas with a lion skin rug between them. The sofas and the lion rug looked out of place—too opulent, in Ciana's opinion, for a library. Still, it was a gorgeous and richly-furnished room.

A middle-aged man wrapped in a red, knee-length coat with gold thread and matching buttons reclined on one of the sofas. Ciana recognised him as Lord Penrith, a rich and powerful rival to the Duke of Onteel. On either side of him were two young women minimally clad in silk underclothes. A thin man in a shabby doublet and breeches was kneeling before Lord Penrith. His head was bowed forward and his shoulders slumped.

Even from behind, Ciana recognised her father at once.

None of the men and women in the library reacted to Ciana, because she was not really there. Her body felt heavy, and she knew that if she tried to move she'd face insurmountable resistance. Thorn's magic allowed her to see and hear only what was in range of the candle in this library. She could not reach out and touch any of it or move an inch from her present vantage point. All she could do was watch.

Penrith regarded Ciana's father with a quizzical expression. 'So, you have come empty-handed, have you Arturo? Do you mean to insult me?'

Arturo shook his head while staring at the floor. 'I have thirty-two duots. I cannot raise anymore.' He held his hand out towards Lord Penrith, a glint of silver on his palm.

Penrith sneered. 'Thirty-two duots is an insult when you owe me fifty.'

'I don't have it, my lord. I've sold my possessions—almost everything besides that which keeps my business running. I have nothing else to give.'

Penrith tilted his head to one side. 'You have a decent set of winter clothes. You have your health. And you have the Duke as your patron. Surely you don't expect me to believe that thirty-two duots is all you can afford?'

Arturo remained silent, frozen in place, kneeling on the floor.

Ciana had never seen her father like this. Scared. Silent. Defeated. She wanted to dash forward and help him, but that was impossible.

Something shifted within her. A slow-burning rage igniting in her core.

Lord Penrith was murmuring to his young courtesans. They nodded at his instructions, stepped over to Arturo and gently but firmly started removing his doublet. He looked confused but didn't resist. Next they unbuttoned his shirt and lifted it over his head. They relieved him of his gloves, his shoes, his wedding ring. When they reached for his trousers, he leapt back as if burned by their touch. The courtesans looked to Penrith for guidance, who was picking his teeth using a pocket knife with a jewelled handle.

'I assure you, my dear Arturo, that my companions have seen far worse than the contents of an elderly spymaster's trousers. Don't make me call my men-at-arms. I fear you'll find their treatment far rougher.'

For a moment Arturo looked tense, his body primed to resist, but then he seemed to deflate. He unbuttoned his trousers and handed them along with his underclothes to the courtesans, who took them and left the room, whispering to one another. Arturo—his skin pale but with the blotches and wrinkles of old age—resumed his kneeling position. Ciana averted her eyes from her father's naked body, although they were in any case blurred by tears.

'I daresay I'll receive a duot or two for these rags down at the flea market. Or rather, my representatives will. I don't venture to such places.'

Arturo started shuffling backwards on all fours, his eyes staring fixedly at the floor, but Penrith stood and marched over to him. He sat on his haunches and lifted Arturo's chin with the point of his jewelled pocket knife.

'You plan to double cross me, Arturo. Don't think I can't see it in your eyes. I don't blame you for hating me, but remember that my hold over you precludes any counterattack. I know how your magic candles work. I know that you have a spy in every wealthy house in the city. Even the Duke doesn't know the secret of your success. If he did, he'd cast you aside and claim the candles for himself. Surely it is not unreasonable for me to demand a monthly fee in exchange for my silence on this matter?'

Arturo said nothing and remained completely still, his chin balanced on the point of Penrith's blade.

After a long moment, Penrith seemed satisfied. He stood up and said, 'Next month I shall expect one hundred duots, plus the seventeen you still owe me from this month. I suggest you use the time available to you to consider how best to turn your precious information into gold.'

'Quite a specimen, isn't he?' Thorn said, rearing up on his hind legs. Ciana felt a rush of hot air against her face as the dragon swished his massive tail.

She was shaking with anger. She'd never seen her father treated with such contempt, such lazy cruelty. Though he'd recently lost weight and often looked stressed, Ciana had never never before seen him display such weakness or subservience. He was a cunning, subtle, skillful man—a chess grandmaster among draughts players. At least, that's how she'd always seen him. Now he looked like a shadow of his former self, a plaything for more powerful men. That he'd been ground down to the point where he'd willingly prostrated himself naked in front of a crook like Penrith was extremely disturbing.

How could he have let things get this far without even telling his adult daughter what was wrong?

'Don't despair, Ciana,' Thorn said, misreading her mood. 'I'm quite willing to help rid your father of this loathsome scoundrel.'

Ciana was in no mood to verbally spar with Thorn; she intended to get straight to the point. 'Good. And what's your price for helping me destroy Penrith?'

A forked tongue flicked out between Thorn's teeth as he edged closer to Ciana. She reminded herself that Thorn was only the spirit of a dragon and no longer possessed any actual physical substance. He still had power, and a wealth of knowledge, but he served at the will of Ciana and her father. He was still bound by the spell that had enchanted the candles and killed Ciana's mother.

'I admire your directness, Ciana. I always have. There is only one thing I desire, as you know—freedom from this prison your wretched mother placed me inside.'

Ciana laughed bitterly. 'And you think insulting my mother is the best way to get me to make a deal? When you were responsible for her death?'

Thorn made a deep, booming sound in the back of his throat, and gouts of flame burst from his nostrils. Ciana flinched, even though she knew Thorn's fire couldn't hurt her. It felt hot, and very real, despite being only an illusion.

Of course, if she freed him, things would be different. His firebreath would once again burn flesh and bone. Which was why she was hardly keen to set him free.

'You have no more wit than your mother did,' Thorn said contemptuously. 'I did not kill her—her own arrogance caused her downfall. The spell she used to ensnare me required a blood sacrifice. She thought she could make it work without one, but she was wrong, and the spell claimed her life at the same time as it quashed my freedom.'

'You've said enough, dragon spirit,' Ciana spat, even though she knew that what Thorn said was true. Despite her father's attempts to hide it, she'd found her mother's grimoire years ago and studied the spell he referred to.

'I'm not seeking an argument, human,' Thorn boomed. 'I want to make a deal. My freedom in exchange for reducing Lord Penrith to a heap of ash. Better to make a deal with me now, than wait until I have no need to make bargains with my prison warders.'

Ciana bit her lip. 'Fine, I'll consider your offer. But for now, send me home.'

Ciana closed her eyes and waited for the feeling of weightlessness to settle over her. It was less pronounced this time, but she noticed as the warm air of the dragon's cave was replaced by the chill of the draughty candle shop. She opened her eyes and confirmed that she was indeed home. It was still pitch black outside and the fire was burning low. She looked for Thorn's eye in the embers, but he was gone.

Ciana stamped down the remains of the fire, hoping her father wouldn't question why she'd lit it in the middle of the night when he returned home from his ordeal.

What was she going to do? She couldn't let Penrith get away with blackmailing her father. Even putting aside her anger and desire for revenge, a spymaster who was at the mercy of a blackmailer was in a precarious position, one that would inevitably end in disaster. On the other hand, if she let Thorn go free, she and Arturo would lose everything they'd worked for. Her mother's legacy would be gone and they'd likely face the wrath of the Duke, whose power relied on the secrets Arturo supplied.

Danger surrounded them on all sides.

Even putting off a decision involved significant risk. Thorn had hinted that there would come a time when he wouldn't need to make a deal with her, presumably because he'd be able to break free of her mother's enchantment without Ciana's help. Although she hoped this wasn't true, she suspected it might be. She was fairly sure Thorn shouldn't be able to make himself visible to her behind her father's back, but in the past year he'd found a way of doing it. This suggested that the boundaries of the enchantment were starting to wane. If only her mother was still alive, she could have strengthened them and kept Thorn in check.

Ciana retreated to her bedroom full of anxiety and fear. Knowing that sleep would be hard to come by, she pulled back her bedclothes and retrieved a burlap sack hidden underneath the sleeping pallet. Inside the sack was her mother's grimoire. Wary of lighting a candle that Thorn could use to spy on her, she instead lit an oil lamp and sat up in bed leafing through the yellowed pages. Although she understood the basic principles of magic, she'd never had a proper teacher. She'd often wondered if her mother had planned to teach her about magic, so Ciana could follow in her footsteps. Strangely, Arturo didn't seem to approve of the subtle arts, even though he'd married a witch and his livelihood depended on an enchantment. Or maybe he disliked magic because it was a painful reminder of his late, beloved wife.

Arturo's return shortly before dawn was announced by the creaking of floorboards in the shop. Ciana fell asleep soon after that, her head buzzing with spells and incantations.

'It seems I may have misjudged your father. When I demanded an additional payment, this isn't what I had in mind. But I can't say I'm disappointed.'

Lord Penrith didn't trouble himself to conceal his desire as his eyes roved over Ciana. She was wearing the same overalls she wore most days, covered in black burn marks and smears of beeswax. It was hardly the most flattering clothing, but Penrith seemed not to care. Or maybe he just enjoyed making her feel uncomfortable.

Ciana swallowed down her disgust. She couldn't afford to offend Penrith. Not yet.

A witch uses her feelings as fuel for her art, her mother had once said, when Ciana was young, *but she never allows them to control her. Anger, fear, lust, revulsion. Make use of them when you can, conceal them when you must.*

'Can we continue this discussion alone?' Ciana said.

Penrith smirked and shooed away the courtesan who had been reclining next to him on the damask sofa. The young woman shot Ciana a frank, appraising look as she went by, leaving a waft of sickly-sweet perfume in her wake.

They were in the same library where her father had cowered naked on the floor the previous evening. Now that she was really here and not peering into the room through the candle flame, she saw that the leather bound books lining the shelves were mostly fake. They were too regular and too pristine, covered with a thick coat of gleaming varnish. This was the library of a man who valued the appearance of power and knowledge but not necessarily its substance.

This thought steeled Ciana and calmed her nerves. She was starting to get the measure of this puffed-up aristocrat.

'I've come to make a deal,' she said.

'So I see. And I'm open to making one. Shall we say that I will forgo your father's next payment in exchange for spending a night with you? This house has some very comfortable bedchambers that are at our disposal.'

Ciana took a steadying breath, and uncurled her hands which she'd unconsciously balled into fists. It occurred to her that Penrith probably didn't realise she'd come here of her own accord. He thought her father had sent her here as a form of alternative payment for his debt, like a cask of fine wine or a slab of salted beef.

'That's not the kind of deal I have in mind,' she said, this time failing to keep the mounting anger out of her voice. 'I need you to stop pursuing my father entirely. No more threats or demands for money.'

Penrith stared at her for a long moment, then smiled and strolled forward. He stood close enough that she could smell his sweat and feel the heat of his breath. He was about a head taller than her, and significantly larger around the middle, so it felt as though he blotted out everything else in the room. Lifting his hand to her bare shoulder, he stroked her arm, grazing her skin with his fingernails. Ciana couldn't help flinching away from his unwanted touch, but Penrith didn't seem to mind. If anything, he seemed pleased by her reaction.

'You know, it's almost tempting to say yes,' he said wistfully. 'You're a lovely girl, and, despite what you may think, I have no particular hatred for your father. I'm willing to forgo one or two payments, but I won't surrender my hold over him.'

Ciana forced herself to look Penrith in the eye and hold her ground. 'What if I said you stand to lose your entire estate, tonight, with a single stroke of the duke's pen? What if I offered you the information you need to prevent this from happening?'

Penrith's expression changed instantly. His eyes radiated anger and calculation. 'Explain.'

'A delegation of nobles is meeting the Duke tonight—in just a few minutes. They intend to propose that he issue an edict redividing the lands outside the city. The Duke will gain new, fertile farmland south of the river Lyn, while the lords in the delegation will gain new hunting grounds and several castles along the Hanspeel border. Those outside the plot—including yourself—will lose out. There is even a possibility you'll be branded a traitor and thrown in jail.'

Penrith narrowed his eyes, staring hard at Ciana, assessing her truthfulness. Ciana did not look away. She met his gaze and held it.

'These are bold claims. Can you prove them?'

'Certainly.'

Penrith's eyes darted sideways, towards the nearest source of light. 'Using the candles?'

Ciana nodded, and dropped her voice to a whisper. 'The spirit within the candle flames answers to me and my father only, but there is a way for you to see the Duke's meeting with your own eyes. We'll need a lot of candles to make it work, though.'

'That won't be a problem. This house is stuffed full of your father's candles, as are most noble houses in this city.'

Although it sounded like Penrith was ready to agree to her suggestion, he didn't immediately make a move to fetch more candles. Instead, he stood still for a long moment, weighing things up. Eventually, he seemed to come to some sort of conclusion. Instead of moving away to bring the extra candles, he reached out and grabbed a handful of Ciana's dark hair. He yanked her head downwards and sideways so that her eyes were pointing at the ceiling. She cried out in pain and surprise and barely managed to stay on her feet.

Penrith brought his mouth so close to her that his lips actually touched her ear. His breathing sounded hot and heavy and loud. 'If you try to deceive me or use witchcraft against me, I'll give you a death slower and more agonising than anything your lowborn mind can possibly imagine. You wouldn't be the first peasant to be gutted and filleted on my orders. Are we clear?'

Ciana, her neck stretched painfully, tried to summon as much dignity as she could. 'Very clear, my lord.'

Penrith held her there for another few seconds, then jerked her head downwards, upsetting her balance. She fell down, her hip connecting painfully with the floor.

As she recovered, Penrith strode to the door and thumped it with a meaty fist. After a few moments, a liveried servant opened the door and stood to attention while Penrith barked instructions at him. Within minutes, servants had filled the library with dozens of candles, which Ciana instructed should be placed in a circle in front of the bookshelves. The sofas and lion skin rug were moved out of the way. Ciana retrieved a pouch and small flask from a pocket in her overalls and sprinkled salt and pigs' blood around the edge of the circle, making sure to not leave any gaps. She lit a stick of incense and left it burning in a vase on a side table.

Penrith ordered his servants not to speak of this to anyone, then dismissed them. 'What happens now?' he asked. 'Do I look into one of the candles? Is that how it works?'

'No. Just wait in the centre of the circle and close your eyes.'

Penrith hesitated, his eyes tracing along the line of salt and pigs' blood.

'It's quite safe,' Ciana said, hoping the tension she felt wasn't obvious in her voice. 'I've done this many times. With this many candles, you'll get a clear picture of the Duke's meeting and be able to hear the plot against you.'

‘Fine,’ Penrith said, grasping Ciana by the arm. ‘We’ll watch the Duke’s meeting together.’

‘No, my lord. I need to be outside the circle to make it work.’

‘Why? Because you intend to attack me with some foul magic while you’re at a safe distance?’

Ciana swallowed dryly, thinking quickly. If Penrith thought she was planning a trap for him, he might kill her on the spot. ‘Very well,’ she said. ‘I can make it work from inside the circle. You don’t need to drag me.’

‘Good. After you.’

As she stepped past the candles, Ciana subtly smudged the line of salt with her foot, creating a gap in the circle. Penrith followed her and gave no outward sign that he’d noticed her intentionally breaking the spell circle.

The library was warming up, and seemed strangely bright with all the candles. Ciana blinked as a bead of sweat trickled down her brow and into her eye. This wasn’t going to plan. She would have to improvise.

‘Now, let’s see how this secret magic of yours works,’ Penrith said. He stood behind Ciana, uncomfortably close, putting his hands on her shoulders, applying gentle pressure to her neck.

Ciana knew that she should be afraid—that it would be healthy and perhaps sensible to feel fear in this moment—but instead she felt only a cold breath of rage sweeping through her, chilling her insides.

'The first step is to find the dark eye. Can you see it?'

'I see only my library and your father's candles.'

'Look closer at one of the candles. Can you see an eye within the flame?'

Penrith scoffed, but then his grip on her shoulders loosened as he focused his attention on one of the candles. 'Ah. Yes, I think I see it. An eye surrounded by reptilian scales. It looks like...'

'It is the spirit of a dragon named Thorn, but don't let that alarm you. He is quite tame.'

'...a dragon?'

'Yes. We are going to use the power of dragon sight, a spell developed and passed on by the women of my family. '

'Very well,' Penrith said, dropping his hands from Ciana's shoulders. 'I don't need a lecture on black magic, or whatever you call this diabolical power. Get on with it.'

Ciana smiled, her confidence growing. She took a deep breath of the incense-scented air and said, in a loud, clear voice, 'I call forth the spirit of Thorn, dragon of the Outer Reaches, Lizard King of legend. Show us the Duke of Onteel in his private chambers.'

A spark flew out of one of the candles, dancing fitfully across the room before hitting one of the bookcases and fizzling out. Then another spark appeared, followed by several more. The flames of half a dozen candles directly in front of Ciana and Penrith grew substantially in height and width, creating a contiguous sheet of fire. Within the fire, dark images appeared and slowly came into focus.

'My gods,' Penrith exclaimed. 'Your damnable witchcraft actually works! I can see the Duke in his study, hunched over his desk. It looks like he's eating his supper.'

In his excitement, Penrith let go of Ciana and moved towards the sheet of fire, staring intently at the image of the Duke.

'I'm sure the delegation is on its way,' Ciana said. 'They'll arrive soon, and then you'll hear the plot against you.'

The rest of the candle flames around the circle were growing taller and wider while Penrith studied the images supplied by Thorn.

'Nothing's happening. When exactly is this delegation supposed to turn up? I see no evidence the Duke is preparing for a meeting. He seems entirely focused on tucking into a leg of venison.'

Ciana took a step backward, locating a hard object in her apron pocket and gripping it tightly.

'Patience, my lord. The meeting is about to begin.'

But Penrith was turning around, his eyes dark with suspicion. 'Where do you think you're going, girl? Stay here with me.'

He stepped towards Ciana and reached out to grip her apron collar.

Ciana whipped out her dagger and plunged it into Penrith's belly, stabbing him once, twice, three times, the blade flashing in the candlelight.

Penrith cried out and stumbled, clutching at his wounds. Ciana darted away from him and out of the circle. She found the place where she'd smudged the line of salt and sprinkled more to close the gap.

'Now, Thorn,' she shouted.

The candle flames—which were over a metre tall by now—burst inward, filling the circle with fire which roared like a bonfire. Penrith screamed and flapped his arms and tried to run away, but the edge of the circle was now sealed, and both he and the roaring fire were neatly contained within its circumference.

Ciana ignored Penrith's screams and focused her attention on maintaining the spell circle. She closed her eyes, raised her hands, and felt the circle's edge with her mind. It was a strange but not unpleasant sensation, like stroking a piece of fine silk. A rush of energy passed through her as she found the places where the circle was weakening and reinforced them. It was working! She was performing magic properly for the first time, controlling the chaotic power of the nether world.

Magic demands concentration and skill, but, above all, belief, her mother had once said. *Believe in your power and it will flow easily from you.*

Ciana applied pressure to the spell circle, concentrating Thorn's flames more intensely around their target. Penrith screamed and threw himself against the edge of the circle, but the magic rebuffed him and he collapsed onto the floor and fell silent.

Ciana observed her enemy's final moments with grim satisfaction.

Eventually the flames died away, leaving only the flickering candles and Penrith's charred remains. Ciana maintained her attention on the circle's edge as something new appeared within it: the grey outline of a dragon, cohering silently like a dark cloud or a shape made of smoke. Gradually, Thorn became more solid and definite.

Ciana looked down at Penrith's blackened body. She reached out with her mind, feeling the contours of his spirit hovering over what was left of his body. It wanted to leave this place but was trapped by the edges of the spell circle. According to her mother's grimoire, the spirit of someone newly slain was a source of great power, fuel for the most powerful spells.

Ciana faced Thorn squarely. 'With this sacrifice,' she said, 'I claim you as my servant, Thorn Dragon Spirit, Lizard King of the Outer Reaches. You belong to me, and will serve me faithfully until the end of my life.'

The smoky image of Thorn twisted and writhed. A sound somewhere between a roar and a scream filled the room.

'Deceiver! I'll never serve you, cowardly witch! I'll burn your flesh and crush your—'

There was a rush of air as Thorn's spirit was sucked back into the candles. The smoky outline dissolved and the noises of protest died away. The candle flames returned to normal and Ciana let out a breath she'd been holding and dropped her hands. She licked her index finger and thumb and pinched out the nearest candle. Instantly, the other candles were extinguished as well and the library fell into darkness.

With the spell circle broken, the library quickly filled with the smell of smoke and the stench of Penrith's incinerated corpse, but Ciana hardly noticed. She sat down on one of the damask sofas, breathing hard, exhausted but exultant. She'd killed the man who threatened her father and succeeded where her mother had failed, taming a dragon spirit without losing her life in the process. Her father's blackmailer was dead and Thorn belonged to her. He was no longer held captive by the fading power of her mother's final spell, but by Ciana's own power and skill. Hers to command, forever.

With the power of Thorn and the candles at her fingertips, a new world of possibility opened up. The Duke's city was ripe for the taking.

REVIEWS

THANK YOU FOR READING *Dragon Sight*! If you enjoyed it, I'd be really grateful if you'd consider leaving a review on Amazon. Reviews from readers like you make a huge a difference to the success of authors like me. Even short one-sentence reviews, or star ratings, are really helpful and appreciated.

Jack

FREE BOOK

JOIN THE READERS' CLUB AND GET A FREE NOVELLA!

As an independent author, the support of readers like you means everything to me. If you'd like to sign up for my Readers Club, I'll send you a free copy of *A Night In Highgate*, a prequel story in the *Jasper Wychwood Chronicles. A Night In Highgate* is exclusive to my Reader's Club—it's not available for sale on Amazon or anywhere else. Visit **www.jackcuranwrites/free-book/** to claim your free ebook!

THE SERPENT'S CROWN

JASPER WYCHWOOD CHRONICLES, BOOK 1

Wizard, bookseller, and real ale connoisseur Jasper Wychwood is meant to be retired, but when an American student tells him about a series of blood magic murders, he can't resist getting involved. Unfortunately, the Office for Paranormal Affairs—a secret department of the British government that deals with supernatural problems—soon begins to suspect that Jasper himself is the guilty party.

On the run, accused of murder, with an undead assassin on his tail... what more could possibly go wrong?

***The Serpent's Crown* is the first book in a thrilling urban fantasy series set in London. Out now.**

Printed in Great Britain
by Amazon

43481006R00088